DISCARD

CUMULUS

CUMULUS A NOVEL
ELIOT PEPER

This book was designed by THE FRONTISPIECE, INC. It was
edited by Shannon Pallone and Jesse Vernon. The text face is
Bembo Std; versals are set in Brandon Grotesque. The cover
and interior also feature Cumulus Mono, designed specifically
for this book by Kevin Barrett Kane.

Cover photograph by Carl Nenzen Loven.

GET THE INSIDE STORY

To get updates on my new books, reading recommendations, and behind-the-scenes details on creative process, join my author newsletter. This is the single best way to get or stay in touch with me. Emails are infrequent, personal, and substantive. I respond to every single note from folks on the mailing list. Sign up here:

www.eliotpeper.com

DEDICATION

To Oma, who risked everything to join the Dutch Resistance and whose courage helped our family and many others survive World War II. She could dissect your soul with a glance and made the best boterkoeken.

CUMULUS

THE FIRST RULE OF ESPIONAGE was the one that the Agency never taught you. Most failed to figure it out, and focused all their energy on unraveling the labyrinthine intricacies of counterintelligence plots. But the savvy few who learned the lesson pulled strings well above their pay grade. The results spoke for themselves.

"It seems our friends have passed an important junction," said Graham Chandler, settling back into the leather couch.

Flint Corvel fidgeted in his chair, chewing on the end of a pen. Psychology books lined the walls. A wide oak desk sat in one corner. Ferns sprouted from a large glazed ceramic pot. A circular plush carpet covered most of the floor. Through the windows, Graham could see a few pedestrians down on the peaceful Berkeley street.

"Dr. Corvel," said Graham. "I didn't come here just to talk to myself."

Corvel's cheek twitched. "I don't know where you get your information." He shook his head. "But yes, Vera called me earlier this morning. She and Huian's fights haven't abated. Vera's very upset. She suspects Huian doesn't take their problems seriously."

Graham nodded. "Has Vera brought up separation?"

Corvel winced and turned his head to stare out the window.

"Has Vera brought it up?" This time, Graham injected an undertone of authority.

Corvel sighed. "Not yet, but she will. Vera doesn't think in straight lines like Huian, but when she sets her mind to something, she rarely gives it up."

"And Huian?"

"Huian is a tough case," he said. "Her personality is like carbon fiber. She's light and strong and obviously a genius. But when force is applied from the wrong direction, her emotional framework turns brittle. It's common among people who spend their entire lives putting immense stress on themselves. It's a psychological pressure cooker."

"You need to ensure that Vera goes through with it."

"I don't control Vera."

"Then you better start figuring out how to. It's time to overload that pressure cooker. I need Huian off balance."

"Jesus." Corvel looked down at his hands. He took a few shuddering breaths. "Look, it's one thing to give you confidential patient information. But you're asking me to use my privileged information and position to intentionally manipulate patients." His teeth were chattering even though the office was comfortably warm. "I just… can't. I just can't."

Amateurs. People unused to duress just didn't know how to handle it. It was like football. The first time you got tackled, it felt like the end of the world. But after running a few drills you learned how to take a hit.

"Dr. Corvel," said Graham, crossing his legs. "I understand your concern about betraying what you see as your professional code of ethics. But I suggest you likewise consider the professional and personal implications of the wider world discovering your substantial collection of child pornography. It would be ever so unfortunate, wouldn't you say? I can imagine all the nasty clickbait headlines already."

"But I told you, that was planted—"

"While I understand the possibility of data manipulation," said Graham, "I doubt that many members of the press, or even law enforcement, have the necessary technical acumen to evaluate the validity of your hypothetical defense. In confidence, of course, we can discuss it reasonably. But I would imagine that your family, clients, and colleagues might not react quite as rationally."

"You motherfucker." Corvel deflated and seemed to age fifteen years in a single moment. "You motherfucker."

"Please, Doctor," said Graham, giving him an encouraging smile. "We're both professionals here. No need for profanity."

"If I do what you ask," said Corvel, "I'll burn in hell for it."

"I've always found it reassuring that the nature of the afterlife remains ambiguous despite the ongoing efforts of religious and scientific scholars."

Corvel looked up at him, eyes vacant.

As Graham stood, a shaft of afternoon sunlight illuminated the leaves of the potted fern at just the right angle to catapult him back into the dappled green of a Malaysian jungle. He had shadowed the principals to a lodge hidden deep in the rainforest along the Kinabatangan River. But immediately after he painted the building with laser targeting, a barefoot boy skipped out of the front, a pair of battered binoculars dangling around his neck. Nikon EDG 8×32. The binoculars were precisely the same brand and model as the favorite pair Graham himself had received from Granddad on his seventh birthday. When the boy raised them to peer at a distant bird, Graham saw himself standing there.

Graham had continued to watch, paralyzed, as the drone strike immolated the boy and the building. The tableau seared into his subconscious like a brand. Even if death was your profession, it could still blindside you. He adjusted his shirt, and reeled himself back to the present. These were precisely the kinds of thoughts that Corvel had spent his career trying to excavate.

"Thank you for your time, Dr. Corvel," he said. "We all make sacrifices in life. Consider yourself lucky that you get to choose the nature of yours."

The first rule of espionage was to find leverage over your boss.

2

"DO YOU UNDERSTAND WHY WE'RE HERE?"

Huian Li spun the worn basketball on her fingertip, savoring the smell of old leather.

"Ma'am?" Richard Huntman looked up at her uncertainly across her desk. Confusion was not a flattering expression on his craggy-but-handsome face. He fiddled with his pant leg, creasing his perfectly tailored Italian suit.

Huian turned away in disgust, the ball still spinning. She gazed through the glass wall, over the tops of the redwood and oak trees of the Presidio, across Crissy Field, and out onto a blue-gray San Francisco Bay. Sailboats, tiny at this distance, skittered across a surface ruffled by gusts of wind. Seagulls wheeled high over the marina. Alcatraz sat in the middle distance, a forbidding reminder of human transgression.

"Look, I know this is a setback," he said. "I wasn't expecting them to pull out at the last minute. I mean, the term sheet was signed. Everything was in order." Richard's voice gained momentum, his words stoking his confidence. "They'll be back. No question. Sanchez will be back here in six months begging for terms half as good. That's why we decided to tack on the extra provisions after

4

the term sheet. It was too rich a deal. They should have come down, and now they're going to back themselves into a corner."

Huian whirled back to face him. As she turned, she caught the basketball with her palm and used her momentum to slam it into the center of her desk. She held it perfectly in place, knuckles white and fingers splayed across the sections of leather. Richard jerked back, and the legs of his chair skipped back across the floor just like the sailboats out on the bay. The sound of the impact reverberated through the cathedral of her office. She waited for the echoes to die. Richard's eyes widened, and he bit his lip before forcing his expression back to blank.

"Do you understand why we're here?" She pitched her voice to carry, and emphasized every word.

This time, he didn't respond. He just stared up at her. She could see the cogs starting to work behind his carefully neutral eyes. He was smart. He saw the 18-wheeler bearing down on him. It was so hard to find people of conviction, people who understood the magnitude of the responsibility resting on their shoulders.

"This isn't a game." This time, her voice was low enough that Richard had to strain to hear. "This isn't some petty money grab. This isn't just another company." She spread her arms wide and raised her eyebrows. "This is Cumulus. We are building *the future.*"

She leaned across the desk and narrowed her eyes. "The future is a demanding mistress. She has no patience for incompetence. And she certainly won't abide a senior vice president of corporate development who lets an important acquisition fall apart right before the quarterly investor call."

She fell back into her chair. "Tom?"

"Yes, ma'am." Her executive assistant's voice came over the invisible sound system.

"Please have Security clear out Richard's office," she said. "He'll see himself out."

Muscles worked in Richard's jaw. "So this is how you want to play this." His voice brimmed with suppressed fury.

"This is the last way I want to play this," she said, cocking her head to the side. "I wanted you to do your job. You chose not to. It can't get much simpler than that."

Richard stood abruptly. His eyes were chips of granite. "Fuck you, bitch."

"Oh, come now," she said. "A man like you always has a contingency plan. I'm sure you've been grooming yourself for roles in a half dozen other companies already. I'm sure one of them will provide a much better…fit."

"Fuck you," he said again, turning and making his way to the door.

She stared at his retreating back in silence as he stalked away. His footsteps beat out a counterpoint to her frustration. He tried to slam the door behind him, but the mechanism slowed the close to a soft click. Contingency plans. Maybe that had been Richard's problem. Even the act of making such plans required less-than-total commitment to the primary objective.

Richard had burned bright his first year, bagging important deals and wrapping new teams and technologies into Cumulus. He and Huian never became close, but they worked well together. He used his vast network, charisma, and experience with negotiation to bring more sheep into the fold. But things had slowed down over the following year, and this had been the last straw. The people at the top defined an organization's culture, and Cumulus had no room for people who didn't pull their weight.

3

GOLDEN LIGHT FILTERED through the oak leaves, and Lilly Miyamoto remembered the first and only time she fell in love.

It was during her sophomore year in high school, and she was walking from a socially awkward homeroom to her next class. After fighting her way through the hallway madness, she opened a drab door in a little-used wing of the building. As she stepped inside, a cocktail of smells enveloped her in an acrid embrace. Looking around, she peered into a hundred different worlds, a thousand different lives. A grubby homeless man offered a heel of bread to a wild tomcat. An aspen leaf rode a thermal as it fell from its branch. The iris of a massive gray eye was flecked with jade. A girl in an exquisite quinceañera dress gave Lilly the finger. A brook bubbled into rapids as the water flowed around a collection of boulders.

It took a full three seconds before all of these visions resolved themselves into pictures. Photographs of all different sizes were pinned to strings that traversed the room in a cat's cradle of color and perspective. Disparate moments captured and reanimated in the clammy claustrophobia of a darkroom. It was a special kind of magic. Not Harry Potter magic with its wands and frivolity. Real magic. The magic that hides just out of sight all the time.

The magic we catch only occasional glimpses of when we're least expecting it.

In that moment, Lilly fell in love. With photography. That day sparked the obsession that would come to define her life. Art was a better lover than a person could be anyway. It might be thrifty, but it was steadfast.

She sighed. Her knee ached from kneeling in the grass, but this was the best angle. Her teenage dreams hadn't included spending so much time documenting other people's romance.

"You may kiss the bride," said the officiant. He wasn't a priest or rabbi or anything, just a longtime friend of the family. She couldn't remember the details.

The groom grinned, swept up the bride in his arms, and leaned in for a long, passionate kiss. The crowd seated in the shade of the oaks whooped and leapt to their feet. Lilly spun, snapping off shots like an overenthusiastic machine gunner.

It really was a beautiful wedding. Gorgeous couple. Groomsmen and bridesmaids who could have graced the centerfold of a lifestyle magazine. Outdoor ceremony at a Sonoma County vineyard. Fresh California cuisine, doubtless prepared with locally grown organic ingredients. Two Greenie families celebrating a happy union.

Even the light was perfect, so warm and honeyed that Lilly could almost taste it. It dappled the ceremony in a photogenic glow that accentuated color and made the scene look like a Monet.

Click. Click. Click.

It was a joy to shoot, and Lilly lost herself in it for a while. Shooting was meditative. You had to forget you were in the scene. The best compositions emerged when your mind was empty, just floating along in the endless stream of photons. Suddenly, there it was. Magic. The shutter would snap shut, and you knew you'd nailed it. Or not. Only the aromatic alchemy of the darkroom would reveal whether the photo would be a timeless treasure or yet another leaflet for the scrap pile. The uncertainty of it all was as maddening as it was tantalizing. The only way forward was to go back out, find your Zen, and hope for the best. Always be shooting.

Click. Click. Click.

The couple made their way back up the aisle. Lilly circled ahead, considering angle after angle. Then she spent some time wandering through the crowd capturing candids before seeking out the wedding party. They shuffled through every branch of the family tree to make sure everyone would have a little nugget of nostalgia.

"A little to the left, perfect! Don't be shy, squeeze in close. There we go. Three. Two. One."

Click. Click. Click.

There were two good parts about a day wedding. One, sunlight was the best possible light. As her dad would have said, you just can't beat the radiation from the massive ongoing fusion explosion at the center of the solar system. Two, fewer guests got truly wasted. The combination made a wedding photographer's job a whole lot smoother. Someone should coin a term for the ratio of good light to drunken assholes.

Click. Click. Click.

A bead of sweat trickled down Lilly's spine. She was always moving, always changing position, always attentive.

The catering staff served lunch on long tables draped with white tablecloths. Each centerpiece was a confection of vibrant color. Wine flowed along with conversation. Matt and Anne cut the cake, crossing arms to feed each other. Then came the speeches. The first dance. Lilly ticked off the checklist in her head. Her contract ended at 3 p.m., but that had been an hour ago. She wanted to get back to Oakland before dark. Oh well, the overtime would goose her tip.

Click. Click. Click.

A hand rested on Lilly's shoulder and she jerked back, almost letting the camera fall onto its strap.

"Sorry to startle you," said Marian, the wedding planner. Her tone was clipped, not apologetic. She held a tablet, and her tight-lipped smile was humorless. The revelers continued to gyrate, and the DJ nodded along with the beat. "I think we've got enough to work with. You can go."

"Thanks," said Lilly. She held up the camera. "I think we got some really fantastic shots. The light was amazing this afternoon." It was true. She had gone through a number of rolls of film, and she knew there would be gold hidden in the negatives. This would be one for the portfolio. Maybe they'd let her submit a few to the lifestyle sites.

"Glad to hear it," said Marian. "I look forward to seeing the results." She looked down at her tablet in an obvious dismissal. For a person whose job it was to manage people, she sure was cold.

"I'll have them ready within two weeks," said Lilly. "Thanks again for the opportunity. Let me know if there's ever anything I can help with in the future." She hated that. The pandering. But work was work. She wasn't going to book new jobs without people like Marian recommending her, no matter how much she disliked them personally.

Marian just nodded, not even looking up. Then she swiped the tablet with a finger and turned away. Probably going to harass the cleaning staff.

HUIAN RETURNED to the floor-to-ceiling window and surveyed her empire. The gulls had vanished, gliding up into the ether. Wind whipped at the tops of the eucalyptus, cypress, and pine trees on the hills rolling down to the bay. At the tip of the peninsula, the Golden Gate Bridge sketched a crimson arc over to the Marin Headlands. Beautifully renovated brick, stucco, and wooden buildings were scattered throughout the idyllic landscape. Many of the structures dated back to when this area was an army base, some even farther to the first Spanish settlements in this part of California. They had aged gracefully through their tenure as a public park, and now served as Cumulus's corporate campus. Some of the construction was new. She herself stood on the top floor of a glass and steel edifice wrought in smooth curves and organic geometry, rising above the shifting leaves like some kind of utopian arcology.

She pushed down the bitter taste that Richard's termination had left in her mouth. The most exquisite classical sculptures were carved from rough hunks of raw marble. He was nothing but a discarded spall. Nevertheless, it was beginning to feel like she could trust fewer and fewer of the people around her. They were too easily distracted by insignificant things like bonuses and promotions. Ambition was a requisite personality trait for making an impact on the world, but money, prestige, and self-absorption led so many ambitious people astray.

The glass was cool and firm against her palm. Had the past really been simpler, or did it only appear so in retrospect? With every milestone, the effort of building Cumulus seemed to become more and more complex. Oh, she knew where they were going—that much was obvious. But the vectors for error seemed to grow exponentially, and keeping the ship on course was a constant battle. At least she had Vera, a constant source of support amid the tumult of a world that required so much improvement. That was precisely why they couldn't afford underachievers like Richard. Leaders produced results, not excuses.

She sighed. The show must go on.

"Bring up Martín Sanchez."

The window went opaque, and a bird's-eye-view image of Palo Alto appeared. The perspective zoomed in, neighborhoods, blocks, buildings, multicolored shade umbrellas protecting the tables of a café patio. A man sat at a table, sipping a cappuccino, and conversing with someone hidden by an umbrella. Two other panes opened on the glass wall, video streaming from a low-altitude drone and from a Fleet car passing on the street in front of the café. These angles revealed Sanchez's companion to be a balding man in a polo shirt and khakis.

"Background," said Huian, stepping back to see more of the screen.

More windows blossomed. Various bios, photos, résumés, press coverage, contact and financial information, social graphs, emails, demographic summaries, health care records, daily activity maps, and other digital detritus built a mosaic of Sanchez's life in front of her. Algorithms excavated every bread crumb he had left on the internet, and reconstructed his profile like a museum curator staging an archaeology exhibit.

Huian smiled. This was technology at work. A comprehensive personal profile of this caliber would have taken a team of professional investigators a year to assemble not too long ago. But the internet connected every piece of information on earth, or near enough. And once that information was connected, everything else was just optimization. Cumulus wrapped the entire planet in its digital arms. It was beautiful.

The balding man stood, shook Sanchez's hand, and walked away down the sidewalk. Sanchez's thoughtful expression was visible in the drone video feed as he watched the man leave. She'd need to remember to pull that guy's file too. But first things first.

"Call Sanchez, now."

As the call went through, Huian waved away most of the windows, leaving just the live video and bio feeds. On screen, Sanchez startled and dug his phone out of his pocket. He frowned. Huian knew the number would be blocked. He considered for a moment and then held it up to his ear.

"Hello?" Sanchez's voice was deeper than Huian had expected. "Who is this?"

"Martín," she said. "I hope you're doing well. This is Huian Li. I was hoping we could have a little chat." She watched with satisfaction as his heart rate, blood pressure, and skin conductance skyrocketed in the bio feed. On camera, color rose into his cheeks and he sat up straight in his chair.

"Huian." His tone was guarded. "Look, I appreciate the call but we're not interested. I already told Richard that and more. We never discussed those provisions during the term sheet negotiations and—"

"Martín," she interrupted. "Martín, that's exactly why I'm calling. I want to apologize. Richard was out of line, and he's been let go. I never approved those changes. None of that needed to happen."

A deep frown creased his forehead. "Wait, let go? You mean Richard's been fired?"

"I don't renege. That kind of behavior is shortsighted, and we simply don't tolerate it. Richard is being escorted off campus as we speak."

"Holy shit," Sanchez whispered to himself.

Her gaze bored into the screen. "I would like to reopen negotiations to acquire Tectonix."

Sanchez took a deep breath and let it out slowly. His fingers drummed on the table in front of him. "Thank you for saying that," he said. "We're honored by your interest, of course. But after what happened, we decided that it would be best for us to remain independent."

Huian grimaced. This was not how it was supposed to go. Time to break out the charm. "Martín," she said. "Let me be totally honest with you." She began pacing back and forth across the office, watching the screen over her shoulder. "We're the stewards of the digital world. We're bringing the entire world online, literally and figuratively. That's why we need dynamic leaders like you, and breakthrough companies like Tectonix, to join the family. Nobody else on earth has anything like your geophysical sensors and data libraries. You would bring geology into our cloud. Can you imagine the implications? We could correlate against other indicators to support emergency earthquake and tsunami response. We could open up entire new avenues for scientific research. We could optimize water, mineral, and fossil fuel management and production. We could roll up all your competitors' data and wrap them into Tectonix."

His blood pressure was going up again. "Yes, I'm sure that's all true," he said. "But as I said, we think that remaining independent is the right move for us right now."

Fingernails bit into her palms. She was glad he couldn't see her own bio feed. "Tectonix is an important piece that's missing from the Cumulus puzzle. I know Richard jerked you around and tried to game the deal. I'm trying to make amends here. Tectonix would keep its brand, and you'd continue to run it as a business line. Just like Fleet, Bandwidth, Security, Learning, Backend, Lancer, and the other Cumulus companies. You'd still get to operate it as you like, but you'd have Cumulus behind you with a war chest."

He was shaking his head. Damn it all to hell. Time to drop the bomb.

"To show this is a good faith offer," she said, staring laser bolts at his image through the feed, "I'm willing to double the economics."

Sanchez coughed, took the phone from his ear, and stared at it for a second.

"Excuse me," he said. "I think the signal cut out for a moment."

Huian smiled grimly, flourished her hand, and bowed. Everyone had their price.

"You heard me right," she said. "I'm willing to double the economics on the deal." The board might push back, but it would be more than worth it once Tectonix was fully integrated. That was the benefit of a dual-class share structure anyway. She didn't need Wall Street suits sticking their hands into things they didn't understand. The board could go screw themselves.

A view from another passing Fleet car displayed a close-up of Sanchez's face. Another window appeared, recording video from the camera on the phone of another person seated on the patio who was probably checking email. Sanchez's breathing was fast and shallow over the audio connection. Stubble peppered his jaw, and he was biting his lower lip. There was a flicker of red. Huian did a double take. It took a moment to register. He had bitten too hard. A drop of blood dribbled from his lip down his chin, bright and incongruous.

The ramifications of the deal were already working their way through the cogs and wheels of Huian's mind. Legal would need to get the docs sorted quickly. She would need to update her talking points for the quarterly call and probably sit through a lecture from Steve, Cumulus's CFO. But once they cut through the red tape... It was hard to imagine the scope of what their data science teams would be able to do with the new fire hose of information. Oil companies would line up to access their ongoing insights into various basins. They could build real-time aquifer dashboards for water managers, and invite hordes of top graduate students to integrate everything into one giant, global earth model. She was itching to get off the phone and kick-start the process.

Muting the line, she called out to Tom. "Get Steve on the line the minute this call ends."

"You got it," he responded.

Damn, Sanchez had said something during the exchange and she had missed it. She unmuted the call and returned her attention to his body language. He had stood up from the table and was staring off into the distance.

"I'm sorry," she said. "I missed that last. What did you say?"

"No," said Sanchez. "We're keeping Tectonix independent. Thank you for your interest and your offer, but it's off the table."

Frustration reared its ugly head, twisting Huian's stomach into knots. "Come on, Martín. You're not going to leave $3.8 billion on the table. Yesterday, you were ready to sell for half that. What's the problem?"

"Richard reminded us why we value piloting our own ship," he said. "It's not about the economics. Three-point-eight is more than generous given our current run rate. But I got into this so I didn't have to work for Schlumberger anymore. I'm not looking to hire a new boss."

"You have to run it by your board, at least. See what they have to say." Huian made a concerted effort to relax her clenched fists.

"No," he said. "That's my final answer. The board can go screw themselves."

It didn't sound nearly as good coming from him. The months of planning and due diligence were all unraveling in front of her, and she couldn't do anything to stop it. No partnerships with the masters of fossil fuel. No raw meat for data science. No geo feed. All because of Richard's shortsightedness.

Air hissed through her teeth. "I've got to give it to you," she said. "I didn't have you pegged to turn this one down. If there's anything I've learned, it's that the world of business can be an unpredictable place. If you ever change your mind, you know who to call."

"I'll keep that in mind," he said. "Thanks, really."

Huian disconnected the call but continued to watch the screen. Sanchez slowly lowered the phone and placed it on the table with extreme delicacy. He pressed both palms against his eyes and ran his hands through his hair. He was trembling. Sweat stained his armpits. He took a few deep breaths, visibly trying to get himself under control. Then a wild laugh bubbled up and out of him.

Other café patrons gave him sidelong glances. They probably thought he'd gone mad, standing there laughing by himself in the middle of the patio. They were right, thought Huian. That was the laugh of someone insane enough to turn down a check for nearly $4 billion. That was the laugh of someone stubborn and reckless enough to say no to Cumulus. It put him outside the pattern she was weaving, the technological mosaic she was assembling. That in itself made him dangerous.

5

LILLY COLLECTED HER GEAR, and packed it carefully into padded, matte-black cases. The meticulous routine reminded her of her childhood garage in Encinitas. Her parents were both expat Japanese engineers working for the San Diego office of a Tokyo conglomerate. They were each irrepressible tinkerers. Her dad's den was an explosion of tools, toys, and materials. It was like a mad scientist's lair chastened by an engineer's practicality. But the garage was different. That was her mom's workshop. Everything had a name, a tag, a drawer, a hook. One of Lilly's clearest memories was her mom hunched over a bench, soldering electronics. The glow of the soldering iron lit up her focused expression, and the fumes were palpable.

Like her mom, Lilly treated tools with clinical respect. She zipped up the final pocket, and hefted the straps onto her shoulder. If she hurried, she'd still make it home before dark. She dodged a few inebriated guests, and cut a line across the grass to the parking lot on the far side of the vineyard's main building.

Night wasn't a good time to be out and about in her neighborhood. The police didn't much care about yet another robbery, rape, or murder in the Slums of West Oakland. The 911 dispatchers didn't even bother saying they'd send a car over if you called in after hearing gunshots. What was the point anyway?

Lilly knew she was being cynical. The cops weren't evil, or even apathetic. There were just too few of them. Far too few. Budgets shrank as crime and unemployment rose. Officers were spread too thin across too many beats. There weren't really beats anymore anyway. She had been to a few of the community meetings over the years. With such a small force, the best OPD could do was just try to keep up with immediate emergency response. Investigations, patrols, and undercover operations were a thing of the distant past. And with Security keeping the peace in the Green Zones, why should the rich folks even care? Nobody wanted *their* tax money going to an ineffective bureaucratic dinosaur. Safety-as-a-service. Those who couldn't afford it didn't deserve it.

There she was, getting all cynical again. She, whose entire livelihood depended on Greenies willing to fork out top dollar for an analog photographer to document their adventures in a format rendered cool by its obsolescence. She was the anachronism. A soul from a bygone era born into a far-flung future. A stranger in a strange land.

Nothing illuminated loneliness in sharper relief than working weddings. The vicarious thrill ride on the joy of others dissipated immediately upon departure, leaving an emotional wake that most professionals drowned with cheap liquor. That wasn't her jam, though. Even shitty booze cost money, and she wasn't going to achieve her dream with empty bottles and pounding headaches.

Lilly's fingers trailed along the olive-green fender of Sara's 1977 Land Rover. It sat alone in the gravel yard. Most parking lots in urban areas had already been redeveloped. No need to have vehicle storage space taking up valuable real estate when nearly everyone traveled by Fleet. She unloaded her gear onto the passenger seat, and then went back around the truck to pull herself into the driver's seat. The engine roared to life with twentieth-century brazenness. She peeled out of the empty parking lot, wheels kicking up a cloud of dust, and followed the country road down toward the highway.

The steering wheel was hot under her hands, and the engine rumbled like the snoring of an ancient god. The road meandered through rolling hills carpeted with vineyards, autumn leaves turning the landscape into a patchwork of red and gold. She imagined herself thousands of kilometers away, navigating the trusty Land Rover into a trackless African wilderness in search of the ultimate story on wildlife trafficking. Or maybe she was descending a Himalayan back road into the Silk Road deserts of Xinjiang where the Chinese government was laying waste to the Uyghur ethnic minority. Instead of pinot noir grapes, perhaps these were the legendary poppy fields of Sinaloa, and she was seeking the ultimate source on the latest cartel *patrón* to conquer the tributary system of narcotics that fed the ocean of insatiable American demand. These were the adventures that her savings would finance one day.

In defiance of her imagination, US 101 appeared around the next bend. The highway was as mundane and disappointing as an alarm clock tearing away a wild and magical dream.

6

"MA'AM? I'VE GOT STEVE ON THE LINE."

"Tell him to forget it," said Huian. "It doesn't matter anymore."

"You got it."

Sanchez's pass increased her estimation of him and Tectonix. The companies she wanted most to buy were the ones that didn't want to sell. And when she wanted something, she found a way to get it. As she'd told Richard, the future was a demanding mistress.

With a wave of her hand, Huian cleared the screen and the glass reverted to transparent. Employees wandered the various walking paths, or rode brightly colored bicycles from building to building. Two interns were throwing a Frisbee back and forth on a distant lawn. A hawk screeched as it tumbled through the sky, wrestling three crows at once.

"Sorry to bother you again."

"Yes, Tom?"

"Graham's here to see you."

Graham Chandler. Now there was a strange one. She returned to her desk and stroked the stainless steel with her fingertips. They had first met right here in this office. His fake credentials fooled her executive recruiting team into thinking he was a legitimate candidate.

The big reveal impressed her more than a résumé ever could.

"Send him in."

The door opened, and Graham slipped into the room. Brown hair and eyes. Face lodged halfway between handsome and homely. Average height and weight. Neutral American accent. Slacks and blazer that would have gone unnoticed in any financial district or airport the world over. Graham made almost no impression at all. It had taken a few months before that in itself made an impression on Huian. This was a man who turned innocuousness into an art form.

"Sanchez still personally controls 68 percent of Tectonix's total outstanding shares." He sat down in the chair that Richard had so recently vacated and interlaced his fingers in his lap. "The board wouldn't have swayed his decision."

Huian sat and stared across the desk at him. "I suppose I shouldn't ask how you happen to know that," she said.

He shrugged. "Richard didn't look particularly happy on his way out this morning. The rest is just me doing my job."

"Our best bet is to wait them out," she said. "It's frustrating, but we need to give Sanchez time to blow off some steam. Once the prospect of a big ticket acquisition is in the rearview mirror, the everyday grind of the sausage factory will make independence a whole lot less sexy." If anyone knew that, she did. "If we buy up some of their competitors along the way, it'll make him nervous and accelerate the process." She pursed her lips. "It'll be slower, a lot slower. But at the end of the day, it'll work. It always does, one way or the other."

Graham nodded. "I'm sure that will work, eventually."

"And what is that supposed to mean?"

"Exactly that. It may work at the end of the day, but are we willing to wait that long?"

Huian mulled the question over. She couldn't pretend to relish the prospect of waging a war of attrition against Tectonix. Cumulus had laid siege to companies before. Indeed, they were running similar operations on at least four organizations at the moment: a nonprofit public health think tank in the Netherlands, two cybersecurity firms, and Disney, with its massive proprietary content library. All of them would add valuable new colonies to the Cumulus information empire. It was grueling work. The fact that she was accustomed to forced marches didn't make them any more enjoyable.

"Of course I don't want to wait," she said. "But what's the alternative?"

"Alternatives are what I specialize in." He said this with quiet confidence, not joking or bragging, just stating a fact.

Huian cocked her head to the side, and her nostrils flared. She didn't like how close this conversation was getting to topics that she *really* shouldn't know more about. Graham's permanent appearance of perfect relaxation made her nervous. But she couldn't deny that he had proved his worth, time and again. She shuddered remembering that shit storm with Beijing last year. He had somehow swept an unfolding nightmare under the rug with nary a peep. Cumulus needed people like Graham. They weren't working out of a garage anymore. They were a force to be reckoned with. They were *the* force to be reckoned with. And reckoning required people with skills that went beyond software engineering.

But that didn't mean he was always necessary. An ace up your sleeve was most useful if you kept it in reserve until it was needed most. Profligate spending quickly resulted in diminishing returns.

"We'll play the long game on this one," she said.

He nodded, serene. "That's not actually why I'm here."

"Well? Out with it."

"Remember Sara Levine? The bleeding heart lawyer?"

"GMO holdout?"

"No, that's Darren Weiss," said Graham. "He's buried in a pile of Thai Green Revolution–era bureaucracy at the moment." He waved the wall to life, and the glass transformed again. "Bring up Sara Levine."

The view zoomed in on an old Victorian house well outside the Green Zone, somewhere in the Slums of West Oakland. "She's the class action maven who broke up Pfizer. She was also instrumental in a number of successful consumer-rights lawsuits. She started out as a public defender." Case history and background files bloomed. "Sees herself as some kind of Robin Hood, fighting for the common man, all that jazz." The audio and video feeds kicked in from Sara's phone. The screen was grainy black. The phone must be in a pocket or a dark room. Carnal grunts and moans came through over the sound system. Cognitive dissonance froze Huian's thoughts for a moment.

"Jesus, Graham. Is she fucking right now?" She shook her head. "Is this how you get off? That's not why I gave you root access, you know."

"Mute," said Graham and the audio died instantly. "All jokes aside, Ms. Levine is in the midst of assembling quite a case. On the surface, it's an antitrust suit aimed at breaking up Cumulus. But she's collecting evidence that goes beyond that, and calls into question the legality of our government contracts and many of the Green Zone initiatives."

Huian waved the glass back into transparency. "Legal deals with these kinds of nuisance suits all the time," she said. It was hard to take someone seriously immediately after hearing them copulate. "They always settle. I'd say that's especially likely given that she's a Slummer."

Graham's eyebrows twitched. "Her history indicates that she's a Slummer by choice, not necessity. The majority of her cases are on spec or pro bono. I'm not sure that a cash payout would necessarily win her over."

"Be that as it may," said Huian, "Legal can drown her in a bureaucratic flood of biblical proportions. Unleash the army of associates. Let's keep it on the back burner for now and explore contingencies if things get more serious."

"Yes, ma'am," said Graham, rising to his feet with a small bow. "If there's anything else, you know where to find me."

"You know," she said, "you are one of the few people on this planet for whom that expression doesn't necessarily hold true."

Graham shrugged in acquiescence. "A poor choice of words. Nevertheless, I'm always at your service."

He slipped out of the room, and Huian spun in her chair, thinking. Firing Richard. Losing the Tectonix deal. Defending themselves against yet another lawsuit. A fresh email from their chief counsel warned her that the antitrust threat was even more dire than how Graham had described it. What an afternoon. Funny how many people aspired to leadership, given its pains and frustrations. Be careful what you wish for. Time to quit while she was behind, and hope that another day would bring better developments. Vera would help get her mind off of these obstacles. She had a knack for injecting a different point of view into a difficult situation, and Huian depended on her for perspective.

"Tom, I'm heading home."

7

LILLY TOOK THE SOUTH ON-RAMP and merged. The Fleet cars heading in the same direction automatically adjusted their speed and spacing to give the Land Rover a wide berth. She snorted. The algorithms governing their movements had little trust in fallible human drivers. Only the extremely vocal minority of muscle-car enthusiasts and their pet lobbyists had kept human-operated vehicles legal through their Right-to-Drive campaigns.

Lilly shivered despite the heat. She understood the argument better than most. The pain never disappeared. Time might dull its edge, but the erosion ended there. The police officer who had knocked on the door of the house in Encinitas had held his hat in his hands, a solemn expression on his baby face. The sunshine of a San Diego County Christmas had glittered off his badge. *Lilly Miyamoto?* She had nodded, not understanding. *I'm sorry, Miss Miyamoto, but there's been an accident.* Her knuckles were white on the wheel of the Land Rover. *It was quick.* That's what the doctor had said. Not painless. Just *quick*.

Fleet's promise of eliminating traffic accidents as a leading cause of death made a lot of sense. Let the cloud do the navigating for us. Traffic patterns would be optimized, blind spots erased, and road rage made irrelevant.

But something about it offended Lilly deep down. It wasn't so much a rational thesis as a gut feeling. The value of understanding the tools at hand. The importance of grokking first principles. The satisfaction of taking things apart and putting them back together. It was something she had learned from her parents. And the way they had lived was more important than the manner of their death.

Lilly knew every part of this Land Rover. She had spent many days lying on hot asphalt, staring up at its innards, hands covered in grease. That's why Sara let her use the car when she needed it. There was no way Lilly could afford fuel, let alone a vehicle. But she could earn her way as an amateur mechanic. And driving for free was even better than catching a Fleet for a pittance. There was a reason old Land Rovers remained the off-road vehicle of choice across the world for so long. They were simple, functional, and elegant in their utility. An illiterate mechanic in Mali could fix a Land Rover. The AK-47 was a blockbuster hit for the same reason. Unfortunately, these days, AK-47s were easier to find than vintage Land Rovers.

Her phone pinged as the highway shot out over the arc of the Richmond Bridge. She glanced over at it and saw an automated notification from Lancer saying that Matt Tobin, today's groom, had just settled the bill on her account. Weird, clients almost never paid prior to actually receiving the pictures. She swiped for more detail.

"Lilly was efficient and punctual. If only she had been a little less punctual about leaving early, we would be getting pictures of the dance. The wedding's still going but apparently she's already on her way home."

Two and a half stars. No tip.

"Fuck me." Lilly slammed a hand on the steering wheel. She been up since six, sweating her butt off to get perfect candids of the oh-so-happy couple's big day. Her mind and body were exhausted from hours of shooting. She had stayed way over the agreed-upon time, and she wasn't even being paid for three hours of driving.

"Fuck me. Fuck me. Fuck me." *Slam. Slam. Slam.* This Greenie prick didn't even wait to see the results before sinking her Lancer rating. Her heart sank as she thought about the number of new positive reviews she'd need to make up for the two and a half stars. And there was no viable alternative to Lancer. It made up essentially the entire market for independent contractors offering just about any service. It had taken her years to build up her reputation on the system, and this had just made a serious dent in her standing.

Now she would have to lower her rates to bring in new clients. Those rates barely covered her basic costs as it was. That's why the only contributions she made to the Trust Fund were tip money. She'd been eating instant noodles for years in order to make sure every cent of tip went into the Trust Fund.

It was her ticket out of the endless hamster wheel of wedding photography and into international photojournalism. She wanted to leave a legacy that went beyond other people's sappy memories. She wanted to follow in the footsteps of legends like Lynsey Addario, Steve McCurry, Jeff Widener, Edward Burtynsky, and Margaret Bourke-White. She wanted to document the drama, the pain, the strangeness, and the beauty hidden in far corners of forbidden kingdoms.

But that dream remained stubbornly out of reach. Years of saving still left her with far less than she needed to finance an overseas trip. Today, she wouldn't even be able to add a paltry tip to the Trust Fund. Fucking Matt and his fucking miserliness. They were probably jetting off to their honeymoon in a private plane while she struggled to eke out a living slaving over shots of their happy faces in the darkroom that dominated her apartment. Marian had *told* her she could go. It was just so unfair. That sounded childish, but sometimes the world was childish.

The steel beams supporting the Richmond Bridge flashed by. Beyond, wind teased at the bay, and the sun was starting to dip toward the horizon. A massive oil tanker plied its ponderous way toward the Chevron refinery. The engine purred beneath her like a napping tiger.

Lilly tilted her head to either side, cracking her neck. Cynicism wasn't going to bring her anything but bitterness. She was lucky she had the gig she did, and had any savings at all. She wasn't selling drugs—or herself—just to get by. Many of her neighbors weren't as lucky. She should be happy for her clients, not jealous of them. Shooting weddings wasn't going to win her any photojournalism awards, but at least it was photography.

Fleet cars dodged out of the way like a school of fish fleeing a shark. She pulled off the freeway one exit early and turned east, following the Oakland/Berkeley border away from home. She needed to refuel, shoot some passion rolls, and forget about the sad reality of her account balance.

Decrepit buildings sagged. Graffiti turned every spare surface into a riot of color and obscenity. Neon signs promised liquor at corner convenience stores. Scraggly trees faltered under the burden of drought. A homeless camp occupied a vacant lot the size of a city block. Poorly maintained asphalt jolted under the Land Rover. She fell into the rhythm of "situational awareness" that her Krav Maga instructors had drilled into her, keeping a constant mental tally of the other vehicles, pedestrians, and blind corners. Nothing made you more vulnerable than simple obliviousness, and vulnerability wasn't a luxury afforded to Slummers.

This was probably a bad idea. Visiting the Green Zone without a guest pass invited trouble. Lilly pushed the thought out of her mind. She wasn't going to do anything wrong. All she needed was the view. Then she'd get her sorry ass back to the Slums. Not even the most self-righteous Greenies could object to that.

8

HUIAN ESCHEWED THE ELEVATOR, and took the stairs two at a time. By the time she stepped onto the roof, she was breathing hard. The Fleet chopper was already waiting on the helipad, rotors blowing dust into her face. The sleek, black machine looked like a mechanical jaguar waiting to pounce. Huian leaned into the blast of air and noise, and jogged forward. A door in the side opened as she approached. Grabbing a handle mounted on the frame, she stepped up and into the body of the helicopter.

The door clicked shut, and suddenly the roar of the blades whirling above her became a dull hum. Bulbous windows afforded views in almost all directions. Yet another benefit of Fleet's driverless vehicles, there wasn't anyone there to impede the view. Huian clicked the restraints into place and heard the blades change pitch. She called up a live recording of a Robert Glasper show, and jazzy piano riffs filled the small cabin.

The chopper rose slowly off the roof. As it gained altitude, the dust around it cleared and Huian could see the Presidio in all its glory. The elms surrounding the building whipped in the downdraft. Employees walking the grounds looked up to watch the takeoff, shielding their eyes with their hands. The Golden Gate glowed in the afternoon light, and the Pacific Ocean was an infinite blue beyond it, unbroken except for a few assorted ships and the distant Farallon Islands.

Angling down, the helicopter accelerated to the east. Roofs, lawns, and city streets flitted by below them. A few seconds later, they crossed the campus's border where a Security officer with an assault rifle hanging across his chest was double-checking a visitor's credentials. The cramped, irregular, charming architecture of San Francisco covered the hills to the south and east, Victorian homes stacked one against the other, eventually yielding to the soaring skyscrapers of the financial district.

Most of San Francisco proper was Green Zone, of course. Tourists could snap photos of Pier 39, and ride cable cars safe in the protective embrace of Cumulus Security. But Slums like the Tenderloin and Hunter's Point persisted, metastasizing pits of anarchy.

Huian shook her head. Of course, not everyone could afford to live in the Green Zone—at least, not yet. Some had no choice but to rely on crumbling public institutions and infrastructure. But it never failed to amaze her how people could so determinedly stand in the way of their own success. With the touch of a button, anyone could access every book ever written, every course ever taught, every song ever recorded. With that wealth of information never more than a click away, who could excuse failure?

From this altitude she could see most of the Bay Area. In the south, San Jose was obscured in haze. In the north, Marin County was a grassy expanse of pastoral tranquility. The chopper bisected the two extremes, and flew straight for the East Bay. Oakland. Berkeley. Richmond. El Cerrito. San Leandro. Fremont. The eastern shore of the San Francisco Bay was a messy patchwork of Green Zones and Slums, polka dots of civic order against a background of asphalt and broken dreams. Beyond the horizon, the pattern of Green Zones and Slums extended to circle the entire planet.

Closing her eyes, Huian let her attention drift along with the tumbling melody and acoustic bassline. Vera had insisted they live in Oakland. She thrived in the roiling medley of hipsters, yuppies, do-it-yourselfers, aging hippies, and ruthless gangbangers. Huian could still remember the conversation from years ago. Huian had been about to suggest that they consider Pacific Heights, an upscale residential neighborhood not far from Cumulus headquarters. But the words had died on her tongue when she saw the steel in Vera's brown eyes. Since then, Huian had come to appreciate the place. It reminded her of the lag between today and tomorrow, the vast amount of work still to be done.

Which was why it was so frustrating when obstacles cropped up. People had such trouble giving up their petty intrigues in pursuit of a larger goal. Tectonix would have given her the bargaining chip she needed to sway at least a half dozen senators. Foreign leaders too—oil states were always desperate to reinvigorate the supply of black gold that kept their oligarchies running.

With a new lawsuit brewing, she'd need that political capital more than ever. As always, the Europeans would blow it all out of proportion, and try to smear on yet another layer of useless regulation. She'd have to replace Richard too. It was getting harder and harder to find good people. That was the problem with being at the top—so many people wanted to impress you that it became ever more difficult to separate the wheat from the chaff.

The restraints pressed into her shoulders as the chopper slowed. Huian opened her eyes and saw the Oakland hills rising up before her from the urban clutter of the flats that led down to the bay. The crests of the hills were parkland, and the neighborhoods on their western slopes were solid Green Zone, streets carving through groves of oak and eucalyptus to connect McMansions, early twentieth century Edwardians, and the occasional estate. They swooped lower, aiming for an exposed shoulder of ridgeline.

They came to rest on a discreet helipad that had been included in the landscape design of the plot from the beginning. Huian unclipped her restraints and jumped out onto the decomposed granite surface as the door slid open for her. As soon as she was clear, the chopper leapt back into the air, and shot off for its next pickup or preventative maintenance stop.

She smiled as it faded to the size of a bird, and then a dot. Fleet was very, very good at maximizing utilization. Their vehicles didn't waste time just sitting around. It was hard to imagine how much overcapacity had been locked into the old system of individual vehicle ownership. There were a few holdouts, of course. People who romanticized the Route 66 ideal while ignoring its deleterious impacts. Fleet could optimize every individual vehicle and trip, vastly increase safety, and minimize wasted fuel and time. What Fleet had done for transportation, Cumulus would do for society as a whole.

The dust had settled. Huian sucked in a deep breath of fresh air laced with honeysuckle and lavender. The Robert Glasper album, rife with pathos, continued in an uninterrupted refrain from the hidden outdoor sound system. The garden hummed with bees and birdsong. Olive trees flung out their branches like classical ballet dancers. Bright-green vines covered the high wooden fence that surrounded the hilltop property, young grapes hanging off them in tight bunches. A thin stream gurgled down its circuitous bed. Flowers highlighted the landscape with contained riots of color. Hidden paths wound their way toward and around the house that rose up in the midst of it all, a minimalist masterpiece of wood and glass.

The tranquility of the scene seeped into Huian, slowing down the spinning wheels in her head. Home. She was home. Gravel crunched underfoot as she made her way up toward the house. Vera would help her sort things out. Ask the right questions and put things in perspective. There was a Fleet car parked in the wide drive, trunk open. Vera had probably just returned from the farmers' market. Huian entered through a side door that provided the shortest route to the kitchen.

The kitchen was the focal point of the first floor. Wide windows revealed a view of the entire bay, almost directly across from Huian's office in the Presidio at the tip of San Francisco's peninsula.

Matte stainless steel appliances gave off a mute gleam. Vera stood with her back to Huian at the massive center island, framed by the view.

Something stirred inside Huian. Vera's thick brown hair tumbled free over her shoulders. A baby-blue summer dress hugged her hips, setting off her smooth olive skin. Suddenly all Huian could think about was tearing the dress off her and taking her right there in the kitchen. That was what they needed, an afternoon exploring each other in bed. Smoldering frustration transformed into libido, steam inside a pressure cooker.

"Honey, I'm home." Huian gave the words a singsong lilt as she stepped forward, gave Vera's shapely ass a playful squeeze, and then wrapped her arms around her. She kissed the soft skin of her neck and inhaled deeply, Vera's subtle scent of citrus and wet earth enflaming her even further. Huian felt her own nipples stiffen, and was suddenly aware of the blood roaring through her veins. The sensual soundtrack she and Graham had overheard earlier replayed itself inside her head in all its transgressive glory. "I missed you," she whispered, nibbling an earlobe. "I love you. I want you. You're the hottest woman I've ever seen."

But Vera was oddly stiff, not relaxing into the embrace. Instead, she pressed her hands against the edge of the granite island and twisted away from Huian, turning to face her in the process. Huian took a faltering step back and frowned. Tears filled Vera's big brown eyes, dowsing Huian's lust.

"Huian," said Vera, her voice breaking. "Honey, there's no easy way to say this." She swiped angrily at the tears as if they were mosquitos.

"I want a divorce."

9

"CAN I BUY YOU A DRINK?" Graham slid onto the worn bar stool.

Richard looked up blearily from the tumbler in front of him. It took a moment before his eyes focused. He frowned in recognition.

"What's your name again?" His words were ever-so-slightly slurred.

"Graham." He looked around the bar. The place was tucked into an alley in the wealthy bedroom community of Sausalito. The salty smell of the marina across the road filtered in whenever patrons opened the door. Grime covered all available surfaces, classic rock blared from an ancient sound system, and old fishing gear had been hung up on the walls.

Graham held up two fingers to the grizzled bartender. "Two Macallan 25s, neat."

The old man poured the whiskys and pushed them across the bar without comment.

"Thanks," said Richard, finishing the last of his previous drink before taking a swig of the Macallan.

"Hell of a day," said Graham.

Richard snorted. "You can say that again."

Silence stretched between them as they sipped on the scotch.

"Un-fucking-believable," said Richard, shaking his head. "Un-fucking-believable."

"I must admit, I was shocked to see you walking out of Cumulus as I was walking in. Huian told me you had been let go."

"That *bitch*," said Richard, slamming a palm on the bar. The bartender gave them a look. "That arrogant, fussy little bitch. Riding her high horse, thinking she knows better than anyone else. Trying to tell me how to negotiate an acquisition. *Me.* I was doing deals when she was nothing but a nerdy Chinese twat in high school algebra. Someone should teach her a goddamn lesson."

Graham repressed a grin. This was going to be even easier than he had anticipated. He was fairly certain that Huian Li had blazed through advanced algebra in elementary school. He also knew that her parents were Chinese Indonesian, not from mainland China. Huian herself had been born and raised in Palo Alto. But once the racism started flowing, all you needed to do was smile and nod.

"Firing *me*. All because of motherfucking Tectonix." Richard swallowed the last of the glass. "Martín Sanchez is a goddamn wetback. He's going to come back to the table crying, you mark my words. Then she'll see the value of someone who actually knows how to buy a damn company. She'll come crying back to me. I'll let her suck my dick and then tell her to fuck off."

Graham raised a finger and the bartender poured another slug. He could imagine few things less likely than Huian Li sucking anyone's dick, much less Richard's. Despite the various quiet contributions Richard had made to marginally legal white-power groups, Graham hadn't anticipated that he had so much boiling right below the surface. If anything, he was surprised that Richard had hung onto his position for as long as he had. Losing him now would likely be a net benefit for Cumulus. It would *definitely* be a net benefit for Graham.

"I personally added billions in enterprise value to Cumulus," said Richard. "Billions. And this is how I'm thanked for it. Can you believe it?"

Graham grunted and sipped his drink. The whisky was smooth and balanced. Richard's ego, less so.

"I am going to fuck Cumulus so bad, the bitch won't know what hit her."

"I could help you there," said Graham. It was time to close.

Richard looked up, startled at the interruption. "What?"

"I said, I could help you there." He looked straight into Richard's red-tinged eyes, holding his gaze steady.

"But," said Richard, his face twisting into a scowl. "You... you still *work* for Cumulus."

"I work for myself." Truer than this idiot could understand.

Richard guffawed and leaned back on his stool, drawing another look from the bartender.

"I like your attitude," he said, throwing an arm around Graham's shoulder. "That sounds about right. But how would you actually help me?"

People always asked the wrong questions. They were so interested in their own goals that they didn't stop to consider what those around them might be working toward. If someone offered Graham unsolicited help, he didn't ask how, he asked *why*.

"Well," said Graham, "relationships are the world's fundamental currency. Engineering-minded people like Huian just don't fully appreciate their value. But *you* understand how important relationships are."

Richard nodded.

"This isn't my first time around the block," said Graham. "I've had friends move from one executive position to the next. But when they move from company to company, their relationships and experience travel with them. Am I right?"

Richard nodded again.

"Occasionally, they bring... assets along with them when they leave. Not stealing, of course. Just contact information, critical notes, strategic insights, insider details, that kind of stuff. Sometimes, they keep that kind of information stashed off-network, just in case. Just to help them remember exactly what went on behind the scenes. You never know when that kind of information might come in handy, right?"

Richard stared at Graham for a long moment. His eyes were suddenly sharp beneath the film of alcohol. He rubbed a thumb along the line of his jaw.

"You're one sneaky son of a bitch," said Richard.

"All I'm asking you to do," said Graham, "is consider what this sneaky son of a bitch might be able to accomplish with a treasure trove of information like that."

Graham raised his tumbler. The amber liquid seemed to glow from within in the low light. The bell on the door tinkled as a regular stumbled home. Jimmy Page ripped through "Stairway to Heaven." The bartender wiped down a table in the corner. Richard chewed on the inside of his cheek and drummed his fingers against the edge of the bar.

Then he raised his own glass and clinked it against Graham's.

"Fuck it," said Richard. "You better put it to good use."

They both shot the rest of the whisky.

A notification appeared in Graham's contact lens display. Richard Huntman was giving him access to a private folder.

Bingo.

10

THE WORLD CRUMBLED AROUND HUIAN. Horror and disbelief vied for dominance inside her, their shock-and-awe battle leaving her emotionally vacant. This simply couldn't be.

"Sweetie, what are you talking about?" said Huian. She stepped toward Vera, trying to take her hand, but Vera shied away. Huian, doubly rebuffed, awkwardly clasped her own hands in front of her. "What are you saying?"

Vera was clearly trying to contain her own internal strife, and only partially succeeding. "I'm sorry. I'm sorry. But I just can't do it anymore." Her voice had steadied, but her slender hands were shaking. "I'm done. I'm just done."

Huian looked around the room, trying to get a grip on a situation spinning wildly out of control. The vista outside the window was balmy and peaceful, at odds with this madness. The kitchen was spotless. Dishes sat in the drying rack. Colorful fruit was piled high in a handwoven basket. The central island where Vera had been standing wasn't covered in farmers' market produce as Huian had anticipated.

Instead, a ballpoint pen sat on top of a single page right in the middle of the smooth granite surface. Huian's eyes scanned the words scrawled along the top, "Lovely, lovely Huian." It ended there. The rest of the page was blank.

"I couldn't finish it," said Vera. "I just stood there forever, trying to figure out what to say. I was supposed to be gone by the time you got home. And then I saw the helicopter coming across the bay." She let out a soft sob. "I knew it was you. It... transfixed me. It hurt too much to move."

Huian felt unmoored. She wasn't wracked with debilitating sadness. She was lost in a trackless wilderness. Earlier, she had been eager for Vera's counsel. Then, she had been eager for her intimacy. Now what? It was simply too drastic a change of pace to take in all at once.

"Vera, I don't understand," she said. "Whatever you're thinking, it doesn't have to be this way. Just let me in. Tell me what's going on."

Vera cocked her head to the side, incredulity plain on her fine features. Then she shook her head. "This. This is exactly why, Huian." She looked at her palms and then back up. "We've talked about our problems for ages and ages. We've been seeing Dr. Corvel for the past two and a half years. And now you're asking *why*?"

"Oh, come on." The frustration was back in full force, confusion condensing into self-righteousness. Dr. Corvel's stuffy, holier-than-thou attitude and his stuffier office. "Most couples see a therapist every once in a while. It's normal. It's what people do."

"If this is normal, then I'm not interested in normal." The skin around Vera's eyes puckered up. "You're brilliant, Huian. And I love you dearly. Nothing has changed about that. But you're so... tangled up in your own head that you don't see what's happened to us. We're a mess, my love. We're a hot mess. And I'm tired of cleaning it all up."

Huian tasted copper and realized she was biting her cheek. Sure, they disagreed on things occasionally. Heated debates sometimes ended with Vera in sulky retreat and Huian nursing the Pyrrhic intellectual victory. Huian was liable to forget birthdays and anniversaries. But Vera was far from blameless. She pissed off important guests with ill-considered political diatribes, and wore her bleeding heart on her sleeve in a way that made Huian privately question its authenticity.

But these things were petty. They were too insignificant to rate such a dramatic change of heart. The hairs on Huian's neck stood on end as she considered another possibility. Tendrils of ice wove fractal patterns around her heart. She clenched her fists.

"Is there someone else?" She stared daggers at the woman she had been trying to seduce only moments before. "That's what this is about, isn't it?"

Vera sighed and her shoulders slumped. Then she pressed a fist into her forehead. "I'm not even going to dignify that with a response," she said. "I can't believe you'd think such a thing. Look, Huian, remember our summer in Thailand?"

They had met at Stanford and had orchestrated a joint study abroad in Thailand, where they spent most of their time skiving off to skinny-dip in tropical waters and make sweaty love under mosquito nets. Huian nodded. "Of *course* I do."

"I fell in love with you that summer. I remember lying on the beach, looking up at the stars, and listening to you describe the way the world should be, the way the world would be. It was magical, prescient even. I've never stopped admiring your ability to not take the world as it is, to see the universe as an impermanent, malleable thing. You wrapped me up in the beauty and inevitability of it all."

Vera straightened up with visible effort. "But that vision is also a prison. You're so absorbed with the future that you don't see or appreciate the present. You don't see or appreciate the side effects of your mission. You don't see or appreciate me. The universe is definitely impermanent and malleable. But it's so much bigger and more complicated than we can imagine. We can contribute to it, but we can't *engineer* it."

Vera leaned forward and planted a quick kiss on Huian's lips.

"You're the most intelligent, beautiful, and driven woman I've ever met," said Vera. "But I'm tired of being an externality. I've campaigned for years to get you to pay attention. But now I realize that's not fair. I've been doing you a disservice. I can't expect you to change who you are. And I likewise can't change who I am. So… I guess this is good-bye."

She was at the door before Huian had time to catch her breath.

"Vera, no, *no*," Huian called after her, stumbling to catch up.

Vera looked back over her shoulder, tears shining on her cheeks. "Huian, I love you. Just do yourself a favor. Be spontaneous every once in a while. You might discover that incredible things can happen when you relinquish control."

By the time Huian reached the door, Vera was already slamming the trunk closed and getting into the car parked in the drive. Vera hadn't been unpacking farmers' market produce from it—she had been packing her bags into it. Huian's head was spinning. She felt like she was going to throw up.

"Vera," yelled Huian, holding a hand against the door frame for balance. "Don't do this. Don't go like this."

But the car pulled around in a smooth circle, kicking up a small cloud of dust from the gravel. It passed the gate, which slid open in anticipation, and pulled out onto the road beyond, disappearing behind the curve of the hill within a few seconds.

Huian sank into a crouch, her breathing shallow. This must be some kind of nightmare. An evil dream that sends your psyche circling the drain of your deepest fears. She would wake up any minute amid sheets soaked in cold sweat. Vera would roll over and caress her cheek, murmuring words of comfort to lead her away from the shadows of her subconscious. Huian could begin again from the beginning. Live this terrible day differently. Press rewind and start from scratch.

But when Huian's fingertips brushed the doorstep beneath her, the wood grain felt solid and real. When she pinched her arm, it drew a scarlet pearl of blood and sent a sizzling jolt of pain along her nerve endings. And that damn Glasper album was playing over the house speakers now, climaxing in a dizzying piano solo.

No, this wasn't a dream. It wasn't an ephemeral night terror that a stack of pancakes and a mug of strong coffee would put to rest. Her wife had left her. The worst part was that she couldn't fault Vera's thinking. Her arguments left no room for reasonable rebuttal. They had been going to counseling for years now. Quarrels often ended in resentment instead of resolution. Every moment of joy seemed to demand a sacrifice in pain. It was like Newton's third law applied to relationships. For every action, there is an equal and opposite reaction. But wasn't that what every couple had to deal with? Nobody had promised that marriage would be easy. To Huian, the lows had seemed a price worth paying for the highs. The moments of frustration were intense but fleeting. In the bigger picture, they were in love with each other. But that very perspective was also a source of pain to Vera because it trivialized the things she saw as most important.

A bee buzzed by her ear and Huian waved it away. She had taken Vera for granted. That much was clear. Even worse, she had thought that taking her for granted was a good thing. Vera was her rock, a solid anchor amid the turmoil of her professional life. The one person she could trust implicitly. Not just her wife—her confidante.

Were they simply incompatible, as Vera had said? Was she, Huian, simply an impossible spouse? Was she doomed to a life alone, bringing pain to those around her through sheer force of personality? Richard would surely attest to that. She had burned many bridges to get where she was today. But sometimes scorched earth was the only way forward. Huian knew she had a propensity for getting so absorbed in her own head that the outside world seemed to fade. But great work required great dedication.

Cumulus. Her great work. The company that she had built from the ground up. The company that came more and more under threat every day. The company that was now veering wildly out of control. Richard's mishandling of Tectonix, and his subsequent dismissal. The antitrust suit trying to dismantle her life's work piece by piece. The new set of European regulations that made half of their products immediately subject to expensive regulatory constraints. The board's constant questions and mindless pressure to prioritize quarterly profits at the expense of long-term growth.

Action. That was the only way out of a halting problem. The only way to short-circuit complexity. If you were tossed under a wave, you might not know which way was up but you had to start swimming anyway.

She swallowed, trying to get rid of the taste of bile. Slowly, so as not to upset her equilibrium any further, she stood up. The world swam around her. She took a few short breaths. Eventually, the garden came back into focus. The lush serenity sparked a flare of rage at the injustice of it all.

Tearing her eyes away from the newly vacated front yard, Huian turned and made her way back into the kitchen, gripping the counter for support.

"Silence."

The jazzy scales died, leaving a hollow stillness in their wake. The loudest sound was Huian's own breathing. The granite was cold and solid under her hands. She and Vera had chosen the granite together. They had toured warehouses full of massive slabs to find the piece with the perfect color and texture pattern. Warehouse workers had bantered with each other in harsh Cantonese. Working with the architect and general contractor had been an exercise of joint patience. They had to balance each other's goals and whims with the reality of design and construction over the course of many months. In the end, it had transformed the house into their home.

And now, that home was broken. Desperation welled inside Huian again, drowning out her rational mind. Vera was gone. It wasn't like their other fights. Vera had never left, never even threatened to leave before. This was for real. Huian was alone. Alone in a treacherous world. Holding the tiller of a sinking ship.

The lump in her throat ripened into a sob that she fought to contain. How many times had she watched Vera wash the dishes, profiled against the view? How many times had they finished a bottle of pinot noir together and let its boozy warmth shelter their tired souls? What was life without Vera? Huian's knuckles were white against the granite.

Action. She couldn't allow herself to be led astray by the sirens of self-pity. She had to steer herself away from the black hole. She had to distract herself from the rubble of her personal life. She had to *do* something.

"Call Graham."

For a few interminable seconds, she thought the connection might not go through and she'd be left to vacillate in ethical purgatory.

"Chandler here." His neutral voice sounded almost as if he were right here beside her.

But she was alone. Truly alone. It was time to take care of things herself.

"Graham." She released the countertop and slowly moved her fingers, as if trying out a new pair of gloves for the first time. "The Tectonix acquisition and the Levine lawsuit…"

"Yes?" he asked into the silence.

"Take care of them."

There was a beat.

"Yes, ma'am." She searched for a hint of something in his voice. Enthusiasm? Gratification? But his tone was as calm as ever.

She ended the connection, and banished the moral quandary from her mind. When you were truly alone, sometimes you needed to address things head-on and take care of them yourself. When the buck stopped with you, what choice did you have? Often, the only way out of an insoluble situation was to make a lateral move. And if there was one thing she was good at, it was solving the insoluble.

Huian strode across the kitchen, ripped off her blouse, and descended into the basement.

11

RENOVATED APARTMENT BUILDINGS, coffee shops, and live/work art–studio spaces emerged from the urban jungle. This was the Fringe, the area hugging the perimeter of the Green Zone that relied on its proximity for relative stability. Residents were former Greenies fallen on hard times, students, creatives, and hipsters too cool for the Green Zone, but too timid to venture far beyond its borders.

Lilly drove straight through the Fringe and under the freeway overpass at MacArthur BART Station, which marked the border in this area. The bumpy ride turned smooth as the Land Rover emerged onto fresh pavement on the other side. A uniformed Security officer sipped a coffee and leaned against his SUV as he watched her pass from behind aviator sunglasses that were doubtless displaying her profile and the vehicle tags on a heads–up display. Lush oaks lined either side of the street, and bright California poppies highlighted the landscaped median. She braked for a stop sign, and a blonde jogger pushed a ruggedized baby stroller across the street, sculpted muscles shining under a sheen of sweat. The next block over, a group of kids played catch with a Frisbee in the street.

The neighborhood transitioned from quiet, leafy residential to bustling, yuppie commercial, and back to quiet, leafy residential as

Lilly drove due east. After five minutes, the rational grid of the urban flats devolved into a tangled web of small streets leading up into the hills. The engine growled as she downshifted to get up the steep slope. The road zigzagged up the hill, the houses getting larger and larger the higher she went.

Every time she rounded the corner of a switchback, Lilly stole a glance into the rearview mirror. It was almost time. The smoldering disk of the sun dipped lower toward the horizon. A gabled roof blocked her view, but before her eyes flicked back to the road, she noticed a little black object zip around a stand of redwood trees in an adjacent yard. Probably some kid playing with a toy drone.

The Land Rover roared up the winding narrow streets like a diesel-fueled bull elephant. If she hurried, she should just make it. She tried to gauge angles and timing with every glimpse into the mirror. So close. She came up around another corner, and a "No Outlet" sign flashed past on her left.

The road angled up steeply, and came to the crest of the ridge. The sun burned low in the mirror. Perfect, an unimpeded view. Lucky for her, the road ended at an estate that sat all by itself on the ridge. She pulled over in a cloud of dust on the gravel driveway that led into the estate and pulled the parking brake. There wasn't much time. Grabbing her kit, she jumped out the door and slammed it behind her.

The vantage point from the road wasn't as good as it had appeared. A wooden fence surrounded the estate. Bright green vines covered almost every inch of it. Once she was done, she had to remember to snag a bunch of the plump red grapes dangling every meter or so.

She prowled the perimeter, looking for an open shot of the western horizon, but there was none to be had. Damn Greenies wouldn't even share a view. Mansions so big and fences so high that they lived in their own walled-off little universe. Shit. She needed this. Her camera needed love, needed passion shots. The minute it became only a tool instead of an artistic vessel, she was done. If she did only paid gigs, she'd lose her touch. If she lost her touch, she'd lose the paid gigs. She couldn't afford to lose either.

Fuck it. She circled back to where she had parked the car and continued around to the downhill side of the house. Then she adjusted the straps and pushed her camera behind her back. She looked up at the fence and took a deep breath. No time for second thoughts.

She jumped up and grabbed the thickest twist of grapevine she could find. Her feet scrabbled for purchase against the wooden fence. The rough bark of the vines rubbed her hands raw as she hauled herself over the fence. She pressed her eyes shut to keep the leaves out, and threw her body onto the top. The top of the fence dug into her stomach, and the grapevine clung to her like the grasping tentacles of a sea monster.

With immense effort, she dragged her legs free of the vines and over to the other side. Then she pushed off with her hands, and fell to the lawn on the inside of the fence. Her breath came in sharp pants. That had been a lot harder than it looked. Movie heroes always made hopping over fences look elegant and effortless. Instead, her face was flushed. Her palms were all scraped up and sticky with sap. Her clothes were in disarray. She clearly wasn't cut out for cinematic heroism.

But hey, she had made it. Time to find her spot.

She surveyed the estate. The landscaping was impeccable. Lilly imagined the months of hard labor that must have gone into designing the layout, grading the earth, and planting everything. Brightly colored flowers accented the largely native vegetation. Gravel paths wove through the yard. In defiance of California's endless drought, a small stream flowed between stands of graceful olive trees. The house was too tasteful to be called a mansion. Some architect had really outdone themselves on this one. Arching angles of wood outlined wide windows, which blazed amber in the light of the setting sun.

Shit. She needed to focus. She could ogle structural masterpieces any old time. Right now, she was about to miss the climax of this little misadventure. There was a slight rise in the terrain just in front of the olive trees where a wooden bench offered a panoramic view of the western horizon. She used the backrest of the bench to steady the camera and began snapping shot after shot.

Click. Click. Click.

This was to shooting a wedding as sex was to foreplay. The bay was a glittering expanse of molten silver. High-altitude clouds streaked across the dome of the sky like radiant calligraphy. Fluffy heaps and piles of lower-altitude clouds formed flying golden palaces. The San Francisco skyline was outlined in stark contrast. The blood-orange span of the Golden Gate Bridge sat directly west of her, the gateway to the Pacific and beyond. The sun dropped toward the pregnant ridgeline of Mount Tamalpais.

Click. Click. Click.

A lavender wall of fog advanced from the distant marine horizon. The tendrils of its vanguard began snaking around the massive piles of the Golden Gate, rising to obscure the bridge in an impenetrable blanket before shooting through it and onto the bay as if a dam had given way. Tributaries squeezed through hidden valleys before rushing east to cloak the skyscrapers of downtown San Francisco. The dislocated flows of fog re-formed into a uniform mass that surged across the water like a silent tsunami. The sun kissed the horizon and set aflame the tufts trailing off the top of the soft expanse.

Click. Click. Click.

Lilly's consciousness subsumed into the scene. She was the hawk hovering on the updraft, the sailboat tacking back toward the Marina, the headlights that transformed the Bay Bridge into a Christmas tree. The tangible sense of *being there* felt when appreciating a great photo was nothing but a taste of how *present* the photographer was when capturing it. Her intuition anticipated how the light was morphing and changing as the sun dipped lower and lower. Art sat at the balance between self and other. Only by fully investing herself in the object could she turn it into a subject. There was nothing but the composition. Nothing but her breath. Nothing but now.

Then a flash of light blinded her through the viewfinder, and she jerked away from the camera, as if burned. A piercing shriek slammed into her with almost physical force, and she fell away from the bench and onto the gravel, hands jerking up reflexively to cover her head. Pain lanced through her ear canals.

She blinked rapidly, but all she could see were dark purple spots. The gravel was sharp against her skin. Fuck. Fuck. Fuck. What on earth was happening? Nightmare scenarios played out in quick succession. Had someone just detonated a nuclear weapon in San Francisco? Was a shock wave about to tear up the hill and turn her into a smoking pile of ash? Was she going to live out the rest of her short life fighting assault after assault of radiation-induced cancer?

12

TAKE CARE OF THEM.

Graham went over to the side table and poured two fingers of bourbon. Swirling the golden liquor in the glass, he stepped out onto the balcony of his San Francisco apartment. The cool evening air raised goose bumps on his arms.

This had been a long time coming. Most operations failed before they had even begun. Success required meticulous preparation, plus a healthy dose of luck. He took a sip and leaned on the railing.

The culture of Silicon Valley had surprised him. From afar, it seemed that the region's success in developing and commercializing advanced technology must stem from intellectual and procedural rigor. Up close, it felt like the modus operandi was, "Ready, fire, aim." It was a bunch of geeks playing with technology like the whole exercise was an improvisational jazz ensemble. But this jam session had vast implications for the wider world.

Graham sometimes felt like a visitor from a parallel dimension. His universe played by different rules. People who vied for geopolitical influence were nothing if not calculating. Every contingency had to be accounted for. Every box had to be checked. Perception often counted for just as much as actual achievement.

The hill below his apartment building descended straight into downtown San Francisco, where towering skyscrapers were packed together like travelers in a Tokyo subway. Lights were just starting to flicker to life. The last rays of the setting sun made the Bay Bridge appear to glow from within. On the other side of the water, the Slums smoldered behind the derelict cranes of the Port of Oakland.

The bourbon painted a fiery line down his throat, and a strong sense of déjà vu saturated his consciousness.

Graham's first assignments had been in Mexico, Brazil, and Bolivia. He had actually shuttled between them for a few years before someone further up the Agency food chain had seen fit to shift him over to postings in sub-Saharan Africa and then Southeast Asia. But his virgin destination as a rookie agent had been Mexico City. He had plied the fraught waters of the VIP cocktail circuit, schmoozed with up-and-comers in La Condesa, and slowly but surely mapped out the intricate web of narco influence and corruption within the federal government.

Upon arriving in Mexico City, Graham had expected he would suffer from bouts of homesickness or cultural disorientation. But those feelings had never materialized. He had immediately caught the rhythm of the place and established a comfortable routine. It was only when he came back stateside that things got weird.

Graham came from a long line of proud civil servants and military officers. He grew up in a middle-class neighborhood in northern Virginia where he played Little League baseball, went to summer camp, and couldn't get enough of *Call of Duty*. His friends in town were in pretty much the same boat. That wasn't to say he was sheltered. His parents dragged him on various road trips to DC, New York, and even Los Angeles. In college, he went to New Orleans for Mardi Gras, and road-tripped around the country to camp in various national parks with his roommate.

Obviously, there was poverty, sometimes quite severe, in the different American states and cities he visited. But it just seemed like the way it was. Some people had money, and some struggled.

A wealthy family meant easier and additional opportunities. If you didn't speak fluent English or if you didn't have much of an education, it would be a lot tougher. But if you worked hard enough and got lucky, you could fight your way up the ladder, and eventually retire in the Virginia countryside.

The countries Graham was assigned to were different. There were two groups of people. An overwhelming majority of people lived in abject poverty with no path to bettering their lot, while a tiny minority controlled virtually all the nation's political and financial resources. The wealthy minority had every incentive to defend the status quo and established an impenetrable moat around themselves to guarantee their fortunes. Privilege was a matter of birth and family. Poverty was deplorable but inevitable. Wealth justified itself.

Of course, it was somewhat more complicated than that. Any sociology or economics professor would layer on all sorts of fancy intellectual models. But Graham's job was extremely practical. Understanding and influencing an organization or society required a bracing dose of pragmatism. Graham had investigated, and occasionally collaborated with gangsters, terrorists, and mercenaries. On the whole, he found them fairly indistinguishable from their legitimate counterparts in business and government. You could find desperate bottom feeders, ambitious climbers, and bureaucratic gofers pretty much everywhere. That wasn't surprising. He always studied the socioeconomic profile long before touching down in a new capital.

The surprising part was returning home. Every time he came back to the United States, the country seemed to have shifted in his absence. Public roads fell into disrepair as private gated communities sprang up everywhere. Neighborhoods self-segregated and became more homogenous. Police departments went through forced layoffs and were replaced by contractors like Security who served only paying clients. Young people were either accelerating along astronomical career paths or stuck in a cycle of low-paid contract work. You were either a rock star or a peon.

None of his friends or family seemed to notice. It was like trying to track weight gain by looking at yourself in the mirror every morning. The changes were too incremental. But Graham would live overseas for months or years at a time. To him, the changes were dramatic. The country was stutter-stepping into a new order. Every time he landed at an American airport, the boundary between the first and third world seemed to dissolve a little more. DC felt more and more like Nairobi. Miami felt more and more like Rio. New York felt more and more like Mexico City. San Francisco...

The city sprawled out under his balcony was a cookie cutter of Slum and Green Zone separated by tense sections of Fringe. It was simultaneously the hub of techno-utopian imagination, and a wasteland of half-forgotten dreams and frustrated ambition. It was a living, breathing paradox.

White fingers of fog rushed alongside his building, and startled Graham as they wove themselves into a soft, cold blanket that entirely obscured his view. In less than a minute, he was completely surrounded. The entire process unfolded in complete, eerie silence.

He shook his head. Enough with the philosophical head trip. The world was as it was. And Graham knew how to handle situations like this, knew how to operate in countries like this. That was why he had decided on forging his own path here in the first place.

Take care of them.

Here in San Francisco, he was a wolf among lambs.

13

AS THE RINGING in her ears began to recede, other sounds slowly worked their way to Lilly's brain.

"Put your hands behind your back!" a voice yelled. "Put your hands behind your back *now*!"

It took a few moments for her to realize the voice was addressing her. She fumbled, trying to push herself up on her side.

"Don't move, or it'll be the Taser this time. Just slowly put your hands behind your back."

She did as she was told and then coughed as something heavy pressed painfully into her lower back and knocked all the air out of her. Rough hands grasped her forearms and plastic zip ties cut into her wrists.

"You picked the wrong house to burgle, Slummer cunt."

Before she could inhale, she was yanked to her feet from behind. Blinking away the last of the lingering purple dots, she gasped for breath and tried to see what was going on. Two Security SUVs sat at an oblique angle just inside the gate. In addition to the guy frog-marching her toward the vehicles, two other Security officers stood looking on with hands on their holsters. Three small drones hovered above the scene with micro-spotlights and cameras constantly adjusting to keep her in focus.

"Hey," she said, finally finding her voice. "What the fuck? You can't just grab me and take me away like this."

"The hell we can't." His voice was gruff, his breath huffing from the exertion of pushing her along.

"My camera's back there, on the bench. It's my personal property." She wrestled to escape his grasp, but he just tightened his grip until it hurt. Coming into the Green Zone on a whim had been a bad idea. Trespassing on some estate had been a worse one. But the view had been impossible to resist. Angles she couldn't ignore. She couldn't lose the camera. She couldn't lose the film.

"Fuck your camera." On the next step he thrust his knee up into her ass, and she grunted as it bruised her tailbone. "And shut the fuck up. Bitches like you don't know what's good for 'em."

Lilly tried not to think about the stories she'd heard. Petty thieves caught in the Green Zone beaten to within an inch of their lives before being kicked out of unmarked Security vans in nameless Slum industrial areas. Girls raped by Greenies enjoying a night on the town beyond the Fringe. Neighbors placing frantic calls to OPD even though they didn't have the resources to follow up on any of it. Security's private enforcement within the Green Zone ended at its borders, but their surveillance didn't. If a Slummer assaulted a Greenie anywhere, it was recorded from five angles, and a strike team arrived within minutes. Justice was a premium service available only to VIP members of society. She dug in her heels to slow the inevitable.

Beyond the waiting goons, a deck light flicked on in front of the house. The reflection off of the windows had deepened from amber to violet. One of the French doors slid open, and a figure slipped onto the veranda. It was a slim woman with jet-black hair shot through with gray. She wore baggy blue shorts and a loose white T-shirt that was soaked with sweat. She stepped forward to get a full view of the scene, crossed her arms over her chest, and cocked her head to one side. Her almond-shaped eyes bore directly into Lilly with the enough horsepower to upgrade the Land Rover. Lilly tried to hold her gaze as long as she could, but it was like holding a finger in a candle flame.

"Stop." She didn't yell, but the woman's voice rang with the polished steel edge of authority. She moved down the stairs and walked toward the waiting SUVs with measured steps.

Lilly's captor's pace faltered. "What the fuck?" he murmured to himself.

The other Security officers turned to face the woman, looking equally unsure of themselves.

Lilly, the guy pushing her, and the woman from the house all arrived at the SUVs at the same time.

"Ma'am," said one of the officers, "I'm Sergeant Chadwick. We're sorry to disturb you this evening, but the system picked up this perp trespassing on your property so we responded immediately. No pass."

"Sergeant." The woman was half his size but somehow made him appear small. "Lilly Miyamoto," she gestured toward Lilly, who jerked in surprise at hearing her name, "is a dear friend of mine and a registered Green Zone guest. I think I would know if she's meant to be here or not. If you hope to keep your job, I suggest you check the system again, release Ms. Miyamoto, and apologize to her immediately."

The piercing eyes flickered over to Lilly.

"Are you hurt?" asked the woman.

Lilly was struggling to catch up to reality. She was about twelve steps behind whatever was happening here. "Umm, no," she said. "No, I'm fine. It's okay, I'm fine."

"Good," the woman nodded as if an important box had been checked.

The sergeant's eyes unfocused as he checked the dashboard on his contact lenses. He muttered a low string of profanity.

"Uncuff her," he said to the man behind her back, his tone seething.

"Sir?"

"Uncuff her or I'll have your damn badge."

"Yes, sir."

Cold steel pressed against her wrists, and the plastic zip ties popped off.

"I'm so sorry for the mix-up, ma'am," said the sergeant. "This kind of thing just doesn't happen. I have no idea what could have gone wrong. It was tracking her as a potential suspect all afternoon and tagged a red flag when she entered your property. But now it says she's been your registered guest the entire time."

"Apologize to her, not me."

The sergeant turned to Lilly. He was a hulk of a man, protein-powder physique wrapped up in uniform. Barely contained rage smoldered in his pale-blue eyes. "I apologize, Ms. Miyamoto. We mistakenly believed you were illegally trespassing on the premises. I sincerely hope we have not unduly inconvenienced you. If you have any concerns, please don't hesitate to reach out."

He reached into a pocket and fished out a Security business card, offering it to Lilly. She flexed her fingers to regain circulation and accepted it.

"Thank you," she said, her voice smaller than she wanted it to be.

With that, the men leapt into their vehicles and peeled out of the gate and down the hill. The drones had already disappeared.

In their wake, the silence was surprising. A garden restored to its usual tranquility. Lilly realized she was trembling.

"I believe you left your camera on the bench," said the woman in a low, casual tone. "Fetch it and come up to the kitchen. It looks like you could use a stiff drink."

14

THE FRENCH DOORS had been left open. Lilly, camera hanging safely from its strap, stepped into the most extraordinary kitchen she had ever seen. It was a tasteful confection of granite and stainless steel, with a layout that would have impressed the original creator of Tetris. She could sell shots of it to house-porn and interior design sites for full-screen spreads.

The sharp smells of ginger and mint wafted through the air. The woman was at the counter facing the window. She was grinding something. The muscles on her thin shoulders and the outline of a green sports bra were visible through the wet T-shirt. Her hair was pulled back in a ponytail.

"How do you know my name?" asked Lilly. Traversing the garden, a thousand thoughts had gone through her head. Relief vibrated within her like a tuning fork. She had thought up half a dozen diplomatic ways to try to find out what was going on, but now that she was here, the words just tumbled out.

"Do you like rum?" asked the woman, not turning around.

"Uh, sure," said Lilly.

"Good answer."

Clinking and stirring sounds came from the countertop, but Lilly's view was blocked.

Then she turned and offered a tumbler of dark liquid to Lilly.

"Does it need anything?" she asked, raising her own glass to her lips.

Lilly took a small sip. Rum. Ginger. Mint. Sweetness. Spice. Carbonation.

"It tastes like a party hosted by Caribbean pirates in a secret cave hideout," said Lilly. The warmth of the alcohol calmed her frayed nerves.

The woman snorted a laugh and raised her eyebrows. "So you're a poet as well as a photographer."

Lilly set her glass down on the center island. The only other thing on the granite surface was a pen resting on a single sheet of paper. It was too far away to read whatever was written on it, but Lilly could see that the paper itself was thick, cream-colored, and handmade. The grain of the woven pulp gave it weight and texture. It was the kind of thing you'd find in an art supply boutique.

"So why did you hop my fence? Looking for a good view of the sunset?"

For the second time that day, Lilly felt childish. What a ridiculous thing to do. She was acting like a teenager ruled by adolescent impulse. Risking a run-in with Security, for what? A pretty picture? Despite everything, she was glad she had recovered both the camera and the film. Those shots were gold and she knew it. She took a swig of the tropical cocktail.

"I know how silly it sounds," she said, swirling the drink around in her glass. "But that's pretty much it. It was just spontaneous. I had a shitty day and it was something I needed to do." She shrugged.

The woman's eyes locked back onto her, as black and intense as Turkish coffee.

After a moment, they both looked out the window. The wall of fog had swallowed the bay and the western flats of Berkeley and Oakland. The advancing line charged up the hill toward them, ghostly in the twilight. As they watched, it devoured house after house as it ascended the ridge. Finally, it breached the fence, swept across the garden, and broke over the house. Visibility instantly dropped from kilometers to a few meters. The window was nothing but a blank slate.

"Come with me," said the woman. "I want to show you something."

Lilly followed her around the island and into a hallway adjacent to the kitchen. A torn blouse lay abandoned on the hardwood floor. The woman opened a door and descended a dark stairway winding down deep below the house.

Lilly paused at the threshold.

15

LILLY STEPPED THROUGH THE DOOR at the base of the stairs, and out into the dark space beyond. Her heart was pounding, and cold sweat had broken out all over her body. She couldn't see much, but her footsteps echoed on the polished wood. What the hell was this? Had the woman saved her from Security only to imprison her in some twisted torture chamber? The space felt cathedral, not some cramped basement.

But what was she going to do, just stay upstairs and wait alone in the hallway? Make a dash for the Land Rover? The woman would probably have just withdrawn her pass and had Security pick her up again. No. The only way forward was through.

The cocktail had helped her nerves, but she was still running on a slow burn of adrenaline. Whatever was down here, she wouldn't be taken by surprise. Goddamn, she had been clueless. Situational awareness. Her Krav Maga instructor would tear her hair out when she heard what had happened. Lilly should have been paying attention to the world around her. She couldn't afford to just lose herself in photography all the time.

A series of switches clicked and Lilly jumped. Big fluorescent lights snapped on high up on the ceiling. Really high up. The roof of the chamber was at least five times higher than a normal room. A whole house could have fit in here. Lilly turned her head from side to side to take in everything. What the fuck?

She was standing at the edge of a full-size basketball court.

The blond wood floor gleamed. Painted lines outlined the court's dimensions. Two hoops with big glass backboards hung from metal trusses at each end, just like you'd see on the NBA feeds. Benches lined the sides of the court. Behind them, racks held dozens and dozens of basketballs. The walls of the space were covered in a single massive mural that appeared to illustrate the entire history of basketball. It was as if Diego Rivera had been commissioned by Michael Jordan. The mural was spectacularly colorful, and painted directly onto the cement walls, like graffiti.

Swish.

Lilly twitched and swung her head around just in time to see the woman sink another three-pointer. Basketballs were scattered around the floor around her. She shot with practiced ease, every part of the motion smooth and cohesive. The ball arced toward the basket.

Swish.

She ducked to the side, scooped up another ball off the floor, lined up, and shot again. This time, it bounded off the rim. The woman took three quick steps, caught the rebound, and fired it back. Off the backboard and into the basket.

Lilly watched in stunned silence. The woman fell into a rhythm. Recover a ball. Shoot. Recover. Shoot. Recover. Shoot. The soles of her shoes squeaked on the floor as she changed direction. The sounds of the cascading series of shots reverberated through the space. In an outlandish way, her outfit made more sense now. The baggy shorts, high-topped sneakers, and baggy T-shirt reconciled better with a basketball court than the manicured garden of a major estate. What was this place? Who built a basketball court underneath their house? They must be standing deep within the hill she had driven up only an hour earlier.

The woman stopped midway through lining up the next shot. She threw a look over her shoulder at Lilly.

"Well?" she said. "Are you just going to stand there?"

Lilly hadn't considered any other options.

"Come shoot around."

"Oh." Lilly felt her face flush. "I'm not a basketball player. I'm not really into sports, actually."

"Basketball is a verb, not a noun," said the woman. "It's not about being or not being something. It's just about doing something. It doesn't matter if you're good. Just try it and see what happens." She turned and lobbed the ball at Lilly.

Lilly overreacted but managed not to fumble it.

"I'll help you," said the woman. "Start by trying to get a feel for how far away the basket is. Then just throw up a shot. You'll miss, but you'll start to get a feel for judging the distance. It's just physics."

Lilly's first shot made it only halfway to the basket. Her second attempt slammed off the backboard and ricocheted into a bench like a Ping-Pong ball. The woman adjusted Lilly's stance and showed her how to hold the ball and the way to follow through. This close, she could smell the woman's sweat and see that her palms were red and raw. Lilly felt awkward. She was a marionette too self-conscious of her own movements. Try. Fail. Try again. Fail again. Slowly her shots started landing closer to the basket. Not accurate by any stretch but at least more consistent.

"I had a shitty day too." The woman stood a few meters away, staring down at the basketball in her hands.

Just as Lilly was adjusting to the surreality of the whole situation, she was thrown off again. Life had turned into a series of hairpin turns, a pulp noir with too many plot twists. She turned to face her, but the woman didn't look up.

"Too much going wrong." Lines etched the woman's face. She paused for a moment. "This." She slapped the ball in her hands. "This is where I come when things fall apart. This is what I do."

"I take pictures," said Lilly. "Sometimes I eat ramen at this smoky little hole-in-the-wall near where I live. Mostly I take pictures though."

The woman nodded, still intent on the ball.

Lilly wasn't sure how hard to press, how much to push her luck. "How do you know my name?"

"Oh, that's easy. The system threw up a red flag when you turned up my street. Between all your profiles, phone, online activities, Lancer profile, and everything else, all your information was easily accessible. Lilly Miyamoto. Freelance photographer who was returning home from shooting a wedding up in wine country in a manually operated vintage Land Rover. Grew up in Encinitas. Parents died in a car crash." The woman's shoulders tightened suddenly. "I'm sorry," she said. "I shouldn't have brought that up."

"It's okay," said Lilly. But it wasn't okay at all. That information was private. A random stranger shouldn't be able to pull it up. "But I never had a guest pass. The Security guy said that it had been issued earlier in the afternoon."

The woman shook her head, eyes never leaving the ball. "When you have root access, the digital world is malleable."

Lilly had no idea what that was supposed to mean. "But why? You don't know me. I was trespassing on your property, after all. Why rescue me? Why bring me here?"

"I don't know, really." Creases lined her forehead as the woman frowned. "Someone told me I needed to be more spontaneous."

"But who *are* you?"

The woman looked up from the ball, genuinely surprised.

"You don't know?"

"Would I be asking if I did?"

A shadow of a smile flitted across the woman's face.

"I'm Huian," she said. She extended a hand. "Pleased to meet you."

GRAHAM SLICED THE BANANA into the bowl with practiced precision, the blade of the knife pressing into the pad of his thumb with every stroke. Then he popped open the cardboard box, tore open the bag inside, and piled Cinnamon Toast Crunch on top of the fruit. Finally, he poured in the milk, enjoying how the individual pieces of cereal bobbed up on the bubbling cascade of liquid.

Graham chewed on the first spoonful with a satisfying crunch. CTC was his favorite of the small luxuries he could partake in daily now that he lived in California. It had been impossible to get his hands on in most of his assigned countries. Mexico had Zucaritas, but he had never been able to find CTC at any of the local grocery stores. He would always pack a few boxes when he was shipping out to whatever backwater the Agency had decided to send him to.

But fuck the Agency—now he could have CTC for breakfast every day.

Swallowing another mouthful of cereal, he relished the memory of telling Francis Jackman, his former boss, just exactly where he should shove his desk jockey bullshit. That was the problem with working for the government. The people on the ground were the only ones who knew what the fuck was going on. But they had no say over policy. The people who made the real decisions had no context, no insight. They spent their days socializing inside the Beltway. How could they expect to understand a back channel conflict over natural resource allocations in Sumatra?

Time to get ready. He picked up the bowl and walked into the bedroom, shoveling the last of the cereal into his mouth. Setting the empty bowl on the nightstand, he kneeled and reached under the bed to pull out a hard-shelled, gray trunk. The lock was mechanical, and he began spinning the numbers to the right combination. You simply couldn't trust electronic locks in this day and age.

The real answer was that Washington fucked themselves and their agents over constantly. It was the nature of the game. Governments were such large and unwieldy human organizations that even their most sophisticated attempts at subtlety usually ended up as embarrassing messes. Buzzwords for seven-second campaign spots didn't translate well into day-to-day foreign policy. The same was more or less true for every intelligence agency of every government on earth. It was just a matter of degree.

That had been the central problem of life as an intelligence agent for generations. Even spy novels got that right. Governments were terrible employers because they barely understood themselves, but governments were also the only organizations with the power to play geopolitics. So agents just sucked it up until they got so frustrated they got out of the game entirely, and spent their time bitching with any surviving colleagues.

But like with so many other things, the internet had redefined the fundamental assumptions.

The trunk clicked open to reveal his kit. He pulled the soft leather gloves onto his hands, wiggling his fingers to help them find their fit. With practiced ease, he unfolded the various compartments of the trunk. *Espionage accoutrements.* That's what Granddad had called them. Graham couldn't suppress a smile. The old man would be proud of the obsessive attention to detail that Graham applied to the endless maintenance the equipment required. Requisite tools in hand, he locked and replaced the trunk under the bed.

While Francis had been spouting a stream of red tape nonsense, Graham had realized that he and the entire Agency were totally out of touch. Like most organizations beginning the long slide into obsolescence, they didn't even realize it yet. They didn't see how dependent they had become on the tools that supposedly empowered them. They didn't see how those tools centralized information and intelligence in a way that fundamentally changed the calculus of espionage. They were living in the information age, but pretending it was the Cold War.

Well, he wasn't going to keep pretending. So, instead of activating the files of dirt he had on Francis, Graham told his boss to go fuck himself and bought a one-way ticket to San Francisco.

He rummaged through his closet and pulled on a grungy flannel sweatshirt and torn jeans. Then he packed freshly pressed slacks and a crisp button-up shirt into a worn backpack. He walked into the bathroom and looked at himself in the mirror. Placid brown eyes stared back over an unassuming, unshaven face. He mussed up his hair and adjusted the sweatshirt so that it rested more awkwardly on his shoulders.

Dressing down was just as important as dressing up. Despite the assurances of the self-help industry, appearances did indeed matter. Appearances could make you stand out or blend in. They shaped people's subconscious assumptions about you, and how they reacted to you. Appearances were deceiving precisely because you were unaware of the deception before it was too late.

Graham scooped up the backpack, put the empty cereal bowl in the sink, and headed for the door.

Of course, Graham had figured out something even more powerful than appearance. He had his sights set on disappearance. Not quite an invisibility cloak, but not too far off. He had performed a number of field tests. Everything had gone swimmingly. It was as close to a superpower as you could come outside of comic books.

But he had yet to experiment with it here in the Bay Area, the capital of the technological world.

People liked to throw around the phrase "the internet revolution." The only problem was that they didn't take it literally. But, to be fair, he couldn't entirely blame them. Unlike Graham, most lacked an intimate understanding of the fundamental currency of power. Unfortunately for them, ignorance was no exemption.

The sweet aftertaste of CTC still lingered on his tongue. Today was going to be a very interesting day.

17

YESTERDAY HAD BEEN SERIOUSLY WEIRD. Lilly ran a hand through her hair as she pulled the Land Rover into the driveway in front of a lovingly restored, early-twentieth-century craftsman house that looked somewhat out of place amid the post-apocalyptic Slums of West Oakland.

Thankfully, Sara had offered to let her use the car overnight after working the wedding. Now it was time to return it, but how would Lilly even begin to tell her the whole story? No tip and a bad Lancer rating. Wandering up into the Green Zone and trespassing to chase a sunset shot. Snatched up by Security and whisked away in the nick of time by an enigmatic plutocrat with a basketball obsession. Sara would think she'd started popping pills, but Frederick would confirm she hadn't been supplied any.

The roar of the engine died as she turned the key and slid the camera over her shoulder. Then she reached over to grab the two cups of coffee in the holder between the seats. Steam trailed behind them, infusing the inside of the SUV with a rich caramel aroma. Billy's home-roasted coffee would grease the wheels of conversation—Sara was obsessed with his brew.

Lilly opened the door and stepped out into the crisp morning air. The sound of birds chirping was an unusual counterpoint to the cranes at the Port of Oakland that loomed on the western horizon. She awkwardly pushed the door shut with her hip. Gunshots echoed a few blocks away. Despite that, right here she felt as safe as anyone could be in the Slums. Frederick ran the Slums, and his enforcers ran the streets. The justice they meted out might be vigilante, but at least someone was filling the void left by the bankrupt city government. Sara was a close friend of Frederick despite the various legally dubious activities of his "organization."

Sara was a tenacious attorney always seeking to take on a new corporate Goliath, and dedicated to social justice activism. Few enough people who could afford to get out still lived in the Slums. She was the one whom Frederick called whenever a political problem came up—managing his organization involved a surprising amount of politics. Lilly suspected they also might be sleeping together. As a friend of Sara, Lilly was under her wing, and therefore had a street version of diplomatic immunity while in their territory. She'd just nod to the enforcers on the corners, and they'd give her a wave. They all recognized the Land Rover anyway.

The house was periwinkle blue with white trim. A gate led along the side to the backyard. She walked through the jungle of succulents that flourished in the front garden, and climbed the front steps. She couldn't wait for the sunset photos to emerge from the chemical baths of the darkroom. They were going to be incredible.

Screw Matt Tobin and his stinginess. She'd develop the sunset shots before the wedding shots. Don't tell the waiter you're not going to tip him before you've eaten. They had decades of marital bliss ahead of them. Their wedding photos could wait.

Lilly tried to use her elbow to knock on the front door without spilling the coffees. But the door moved at her touch. It must have been left slightly ajar.

"Sara?" Lilly nudged the door fully open with her shoulder and stepped through into the living room.

Both coffee cups fell from her hands and exploded when they hit the floor, steaming liquid pouring out over polished hardwood.

Sara lay over the arm of the couch. A gory crater oozed blood from where her right eye used to be. Another bullet had burrowed through her left breast, making a scarlet mess of her white cashmere sweater. Limbs hung at awkward angles. Curly brown hair fanned out across the cushion. Her mouth hung slightly open, jaw slack. Blood had seeped into the leather and splattered onto the piles of paperwork on the coffee table.

Lilly couldn't scream. It was like all the air had been sucked out of the room. Her mind and muscles were locked in abject shock.

And it was because she couldn't scream that she heard the gentle jingle of the bell attached to the property's side gate.

18

ADRENALINE WAS THE NECTAR OF THE GODS. The cold rush of it slowed time, sharpened the senses, and accelerated the heart. Adrenaline brought the world into focus and injected urgency into the otherwise mundane. It had been too long since Graham Chandler had tasted that sweet ambrosia. Now, he relished it.

He smiled despite himself. The graffiti scrawled across the brick wall next to him was brighter. The relaxed rhythm of his shoes hitting the sidewalk was sharper. The smell of jasmine from the vines entangling a nearby fence was sweeter.

Anticipating the young thugs hanging out on the corner outside the liquor store, he crossed the street and kept his eyes down. He could take them down in his sleep, of course. They were nothing more than high-school dropouts with egos inflated by the pistols tucked into their waistbands.

Graham had seen their kind all over the world. Young men with no prospects made for great recruits. When you had no role models and no path to employment or opportunity, there was only one option. Mafiosi. Sicarios. ISIS. They flowed from the same source. All their enlisted men had an identical, sour funk of sweat, testosterone, and desperation.

He could kill or disable them before they even realized what was happening. But that wasn't why he was here. He had more important targets than street-level flunkies. Everything was falling into place. This morning had gone well. Quick. Clean. Efficient. Now it was all about the segue. A smooth exit to stage right. Scene.

So, for now, he was just another Slummer trying to get by. No need to draw attention.

He cut right at the next corner and headed for the West Oakland BART Station. Cheap prostitutes were already lounging on the corners. A homeless guy with beet-red eyes worked on his morning dose of malt liquor. Shattered glass peppered the sidewalk. A squad of gangsters pedaled by on BMX bikes, hurling insults at each other.

Graham felt just as comfortable here as in the gilded conference rooms of the elite. Hell, it was a serious step up from running ops in godforsaken Mindanao. Even the most poverty-stricken parts of the United States didn't have endemic dengue and spiders bigger than your hand. He should have made the jump years ago.

He would have made the jump years ago if it hadn't been for Granddad. Granddad, with his relentless dedication to an institution that had long forgotten him. What was loyalty worth when the people in charge were so incompetent that they undermined your life's work? But despite the monstrous ineptitude in Washington, Granddad had stayed tenaciously loyal to the Agency right through to the end. They had erased all the records of what he had accomplished in Guatemala, Chiapas, Congo, and Kyrgyzstan. He had paved their path to power, and they had reciprocated by fencing him off in a bureaucratic labyrinth of nondisclosure and deniability. But they couldn't sway his fierce dedication to a forgotten ideal, an American dream fading into the mists of history.

The smile soured. It was a blessing Granddad hadn't survived to see Graham leave the Agency. He must be turning over in his grave right now.

"Black," said Graham.

The street vendor was a hunched old man stirring a cauldron of coffee over a spitting Bunsen burner. He dipped a battered tin camping mug into the bumbling pot and offered it up. Graham approved the digital payment and accepted the steaming cup. The thick, bitter brew reminded him of his last official op in Aceh, Indonesia.

He had spent months mapping out the byzantine deals made in the hundreds of tiny cafés around the city. The coffee there had been just as viscous but impossibly sweet. Everyone had an agenda, and most had at least two. International oil companies vied for competitive advantage. Traffickers of anything and everything played cat and mouse with authorities in the Malacca Strait. Government officials from Jakarta whored out their country's impressive stock of natural resources for pennies on the dollar. The Indians, the Chinese, and the Americans fought a shadow war for geopolitical influence while the Singaporeans tried to play all sides against each other. Even the Dutch still had a presence, unwilling to allow their historic colony to give up the ghost entirely. Some things never changed. Until they did.

The moment hung crystal clear in Graham's memory. Walking into the suite in the boutique hotel on that secluded beach on Pulau Weh, a tiny island off the northern tip of Sumatra. The five men so intent on their game of poker that they didn't even realize that the room service they had ordered was being delivered by a *bule*, a white foreigner. Lifting the gleaming lid of the silver platter to reveal a matte-black Beretta M9. The muffled pops of the silenced weapon as he double-tapped each scheming motherfucker in the head.

The ensuing coup handed Washington the strings. Only it turned out that the White House was too scared to play puppeteer anymore. The Agency should have pinned a Distinguished Intelligence Medal on him the moment he landed. Instead, his boss had ripped him a new one courtesy of the sitting president.

No wonder this country was falling apart.

Graham swigged the dregs, returned the mug, and thanked the vendor.

He had read the writing on the wall. All respect to Granddad, but Graham wasn't about to be banished to a Langley cubicle. No. The back office wasn't for him. His place was in the field, and he was, finally, his own man.

The geography of geopolitics was changing, and the folks in the corner office didn't even realize what was happening. It was funny, in a pathetic kind of way. Washington was so caught up in its own intrigue that the players forgot the literal basis of the power they wielded. Letting corporate tycoons pad your campaign coffers was a respected form of corruption. But follow that line to its inevitable conclusion, and it changed who was beholden to whom. Bribes were investments, not gifts. Those investments paid themselves off with favorable policies, government contracts, and a friendly ear inside the White House. Suddenly the people making the real decisions didn't even live in Washington. They delegated *to* Washington.

Graham shook his head as he passed through the ticket gate and climbed the stairs up to the platform. American politicians had made the ultimate mistake. They weren't playing the long game. Instead, they tripped over each other chasing votes and polls and contributions.

The train screeched along the raised tracks as it approached the platform. It jerked to a stop, and Graham entered and found a seat. The stained floor smelled faintly of vomit, and death metal was blasting from a portable boom box halfway down the car.

BART was a perfect example. It had been built in the 1960s to serve a growing Bay Area, and had been neglected ever since. Now, only Slummers used the crumbling public transportation system. Anyone who could afford it traveled via Fleet. Like so many other things, leadership and control of previously public infrastructure had been ceded to the private sector. No. Not just the private sector. Cumulus.

Venture capitalists weren't the only ones riding the wave of accelerating technological innovation. New tools were all well and good. But Graham knew that these new tools gave their makers extraordinary power. That is what the laggards in Washington didn't understand.

Software was eating the world. Whoever controlled software controlled the world. Whoever controlled the world needed people like Graham, whether they liked it or not.

He had to give Sara Levine credit. The bitch didn't even beg for her life. He slipped through the door, and she looked up from the paperwork scattered across the coffee table in front of her. Only lawyers still used physical paper in that kind of quantity. She immediately moved to run, but he was ready for it and had the Beretta trained on her before she could get to her feet. Once she could see the game was up, she didn't scream. She just half smiled this sardonic little smile, daring him to live up to her expectations.

But Graham hadn't gotten to where he was today by giving in to sentimentality. You didn't harass tech giants if you weren't prepared to play in the big leagues. Sara should have known better than to file a nuisance suit that threatened to break up Cumulus. Of course, he had anonymously leaked her the key information about Cumulus that made her case a viable threat. Otherwise, there wouldn't have been a need to eliminate her, and he would have remained outside Huian's circle of trust. Powerful people were the easiest to manipulate because they had the most to lose.

Sara's smile had disappeared when he put one bullet through her right eye and another through her heart. Oh, the rush. He patted his pocket and felt the miniature camcorder recording through a faux button. The pieces were falling into place. Intrigue was its own special class of narcotic. A fresh surge of adrenaline pumped through Graham's veins at the thought of it.

His day was just getting started.

19

TWO SECURITY OFFICERS looked Graham up and down as he disembarked and crossed over into the North Berkeley Green Zone. They could see his digital credentials outclassed them by many orders of magnitude, so they moved on to harass someone else. They probably thought he was returning from a long night indulging in Slum pussy. If they checked back through their feed later, they wouldn't even be able to locate the record of his passing.

Time to shift gears.

He found a quiet espresso bar and ordered a macchiato. While the barista was preparing it, Graham slipped off into the bathroom and changed into the clothes he carried in his backpack. He carefully reinstalled the camcorder and stuffed the scummy garb into the backpack. He had entered the bathroom as a down-and-out Slummer and exited as a polished Greenie businessman.

The barista almost didn't recognize him when Graham claimed his macchiato.

Graham sipped from the paper cup as he strolled along the shaded sidewalk lined by maples. Parents hustled their kids into waiting Fleets, haranguing them about being late for school. Everyone was so used to living in a bubble that they didn't even bother to think about how easily bubbles popped. A photographer was taking pictures of the fall colors on the other side of the street. Autumn had turned the leaves into a fiery patchwork, and a morning breeze set them dancing. It had been a dry spring, and the Bay Area was suffering through another prolonged drought. But here in the Green Zone, the manicured trees and shrubs weren't in any danger. Automated irrigation systems kept them verdant in the face of nature's thrift.

A redheaded jogger ran by with a golden retriever at her side, cheeks flushed and breasts bouncing. He stole a quick glance over his shoulder to check out her spandex-wrapped ass as she continued down the block. It had been too long. Maybe he should have made good on the assumption of those Security guys and gotten himself laid last night. There were many things he loved about his chosen profession, but the permanent bachelor status wasn't one of them.

Hollywood gave its spies a constant string of one-night stands with supermodels. That was where the James Bond movies deviated from the books. Cinematic 007 enjoyed his sexual escapades with the enthusiasm of a frat boy on spring break. Literary 007 was wracked by depression, and sex offered him little more than a tantalizing-but-brief distraction from the inherent loneliness of his job. Fleming had gotten a lot wrong about espionage, but he had nailed that last part.

Graham crumpled up the paper cup and tossed it into a bin. Enough. He was here by choice, and he would suffer the consequences.

Speaking of here, he had arrived.

The office was a small two-story building that had been recently reshingled. Redwood trees rose around it, lending the space a calm, arboreal feel. Graham walked past it, and then doubled back. He brought up a feed on his contact lens display that showed Dr. Flint Corvel's calendar of appointments. Perfect, he was just finishing up with his first patient. Graham reached into the system and shifted the next appointment on the calendar, replacing it with a pseudonym. The change would propagate through the system and automatically reschedule the person in question, doubtless pissing them off. Given the rates that Corvel charged, they had a right to be angry. But that wasn't Graham's problem. To put it more precisely, Graham was Corvel's problem.

The door opened at his touch, and Graham climbed the stairs to the waiting room. A few minutes later, a flustered-looking middle-aged woman emerged from the office, ignoring Graham.

"Mr. Ganges?"

Corvel's balding head poked out of the office door. He was clearly surprised at having a new patient whom he hadn't noticed coming up in his calendar. When he saw Graham seated there with his legs crossed, Corvel's face froze.

"You." His inflection dripped pure hatred.

Graham rose to his feet and nodded. "In the flesh."

Corvel placed his short portly frame in the middle of the doorway, blocking Graham's path into the office.

"What happened to Erica? I was supposed to see her now."

"I'm sure Ms. Edelman will find a convenient time to reschedule her appointment."

"I told you not to come here again," he said, fists clenched. "Ever. I was explicit."

"My good doctor," said Graham. "I'm afraid you may misunderstand the nature of our relationship. Which, to be frank, I find quite ironic given the nature of your expertise."

"Stop fucking with me," said Corvel, his voice high and thin. "Get out of here. I don't ever want to see your face in my office."

Graham could almost appreciate his attempt at toughness. Almost.

"When you are working with a patient who is skirting the edge of sanity," said Graham, "do you find that there is a point, a very special point, when they just *snap?*"

Graham snapped his fingers to illustrate the point, and Corvel nearly jumped out of his skin. Graham rose to his feet and put his hand on the man's shoulder, which trembled at his touch.

"I am here for a very simple reason," said Graham, smiling like a proud uncle. "To congratulate you on your good work," he held up a finger, "and to remind you who your true friends are."

Corvel's face looked like he had just swallowed sour milk.

Graham patted his cheek and turned toward the door.

20

IN RETROSPECT, she probably shouldn't have followed him.

Lilly walked through the BART ticket gate, trying to keep at least a few other people between her and the man. He had unruly brown hair and wore a loose flannel sweatshirt over torn jeans. A nondescript backpack hung from his shoulder.

She had snapped his picture through Sara's living room window, her friend's corpse splayed out on the couch behind her. What were you supposed to do when you discovered your friend had been murdered? She could have called the police, but they would have taken ages to respond. She could have called that beefy sergeant from Security, but he was just as likely to arrest her as listen to her.

But this man had been strolling out the side gate of Sara's backyard like it was the most normal thing in the world. Lilly had never seen him before, and Sara lived alone. He had to be the killer. Remembering the camera dangling around her neck, she snatched it up to get a shot of him through the window. But by the time she had it ready, the angle was bad and she couldn't see his face. She took the shot and then dashed out through the back, noting that the back door was closed but unlocked. She made it through the side gate just in time to see him round a corner at the end of the block.

Strolling through the neighborhood streets to the station, he looked like just another Slummer. She stayed at least a block behind, crouching behind an overflowing dumpster while he purchased a morning coffee from a street vendor. He moved on, and it was clear he was headed for BART. She had to tighten the gap to make sure she didn't lose him in the crowd of people entering and exiting the station.

She stepped onto the escalator once he was a third of the way up. Keeping her camera down in front of her chest, she angled the lens up and took a picture as he stepped off the escalator and onto the platform. His face had flashed past for a moment, but she doubted she had gotten a good shot off.

Every BART car had two sets of doors—one near the front, and one near the rear. He stood waiting for the Richmond train. When it arrived, she entered into the same car through the other door.

Lilly's entire body was trembling. Who was this man? Why had he killed Sara? Was she insane to have followed him this far? But if she didn't, wouldn't he just get away? The cops probably wouldn't have shown up until that afternoon. By that time, he would have been long gone. She gripped her camera tight—at least she'd have some evidence to show for it once she got in touch with the police. Pretending to fuss with it, she fired off shots in his direction whenever the train screeched loud enough to cover the sound of the shutter.

He disembarked in North Berkeley, and she followed him past a couple of Security guards. Her guest pass was still valid so they didn't harass her, but there was no way she would trust them to take her side if she reported the murder. For a moment, she was afraid they'd sense her fear and approach her, but they didn't give her a second look.

Out on the street in the North Berkeley Green Zone, Lilly rounded a corner just in time to see the man duck into a café. She crossed the street and sat on a park bench, pretending to watch the foot traffic. Every time the café door opened, her eyes would dart over to see who was leaving.

She couldn't stop her hands from shaking no matter how hard she tried. Sara's empty eye socket stared back at her whenever she blinked. It was too much to take in. They had gossiped over a late-night glass of wine the night before last, when Sara had offered to let Lilly use the Land Rover for the Tobin wedding. Now her bodily fluids covered half the living room. The two mental images just couldn't exist in the same universe.

She almost missed him. The man looked completely different. The grungy sweatshirt and jeans were gone, replaced by a crisp buttoned shirt and slacks. It was the hair that tipped her off. The brown rumpled locks still stuck out at odd angles. She did a double take and then paralleled his path by walking up the opposite side of the street.

Within a few blocks, they entered a residential neighborhood. The maples lining the sidewalk had leaves the color of blood. At least they gave Lilly the convenient excuse of photographing the trees. The man glanced back to check out a passing jogger, and Lilly got a decent shot of his face.

At this point, momentum was the only thing keeping her going. Panic had sparked her into action instead of freezing her up. Now she couldn't stop for fear of falling into its paralyzing embrace.

On the opposite sidewalk, the man spun on his heels and headed back up the sidewalk, veering off to enter a small, shingled office building.

Lilly forced herself to continue up the block before doubling back. An aggressive bougainvillea bush bursting out of a neighbor's yard gave her partial cover as she zoomed in on the building through her lens. A small sign near the door read, "Flint Corvel, PhD Psychologist, Private Practice." A blonde woman who looked to be in her fifties came out the door and hopped into a waiting Fleet, which accelerated off down the road.

A honeybee buzzed by Lilly's ear and she waved it away. Standing here under the bougainvillea, smelling the fresh-cut grass of an irrigated Greenie lawn, her thoughts began to settle into a semblance of rationality. She wasn't a hard-boiled detective or private eye out of some noir graphic novel. She was a photographer. A *wedding* photographer. Sara had just been brutally murdered. Lilly shouldn't be shadowing a suspect. She should let someone know. Someone who would know what to do in situations like this. Start with the police, go from there.

The office building door opened again, and the man emerged. She had a perfect angle on his face. Raising the camera, she snapped a shot. She clicked the shutter button again, but it didn't open. Shit. It was out of film. There was no time to replace it with a new roll. She snatched her phone from her pocket and used her fingers to adjust the digital camera to maximum zoom. Then she tapped the screen repeatedly to take a series of shots as the man walked up the path from the building to the sidewalk.

"Error: photos could not be saved." The message popped up in the middle of her screen. She dismissed the notification and took another rapid-fire series of shots.

"Error: photos could not be saved." What the hell? Her battery was fine, and the phone displayed a strong Bandwidth connection. Again, she tried to snap a few more.

"Error: photos could not be saved."

Fuck. He was crossing the street and approaching her corner. She heard the soft growl of an engine, and a Fleet pulled up to the curb next to her. Her pulse pounded in her ears. She lowered her phone and pretended to text, pulling down a bougainvillea flower to her nose as a weak last-minute cover for her presence.

"Hi."

She looked up, and the man was standing right there in front of her. He smiled. Brown eyes stared down from a face that could have be anywhere between thirty-five and fifty years old. She thought she might have a heart attack.

She nodded back, not trusting herself to speak.

"I apologize if this is a little forward," he said. "But I think you've got a killer sense of style."

So this was what it felt like to be hit on by a hit man.

21

ANYTHING THAT CAN GO WRONG WILL GO WRONG.

Murphy's Law was a bitch, especially because it was impossible to know whether or not you were anticipating all the things that could go wrong. As a matter of fact, you were pretty much guaranteed to be missing something.

Like yesterday, for example. Huian's head of corporate development had fumbled a critical deal and proved himself to be a blithering idiot, forcing her to fire him. Said deal had stubbornly remained off the table thanks to Martín's headstrong bid for independence. And a nuisance suit had skyrocketed from minor irritant to major liability threat. One could argue that all of that was par for the course, given that she was CEO of Cumulus. Thankfully, she had Graham to rely on. More and more, it felt like he was the only one she could depend on to actually get the job done. Her other lieutenants just hadn't been producing results. Trust was the rarest of commodities.

But Vera asking for a divorce? That had blindsided her, even if Vera said it shouldn't have. Sure, they had been seeing Dr. Corvel for a while now. But he wrapped everything in so many psychobabble buzzwords that Huian had stopped taking him seriously ages ago. Him and his damn bald spot. Whenever they were in his office, she couldn't keep her eyes off it.

It told you a lot about your day when discovering someone trespassing on your property was the high point. Lilly. Lilly Miyamoto. There was something about her frank gaze, her unnerving sense of presence and practicality. Huian couldn't help but find her fascinating. Her leather jacket, tank top, gray canvas pants, and boots were all very worn, but of high-quality manufacture. Thick black-framed glasses slightly enlarged her eyes. She looked like some kind of cyberpunk nomad with an aversion to technology. Or maybe she had found her entire wardrobe at the estate sale of a 1940s-era archaeologist.

Regardless, Lilly was... different. Different from the industrious engineers, scheming attorneys, and ambitious businesspeople who made up Huian's social circle. To be honest, her social circle had an embarrassingly large overlap with her professional circle, which meant Cumulus.

That was one of the things that had frustrated Vera. She had always complained that Huian conflated her personal and professional lives. But that was because, even after years of living together, Vera still failed to understand how important Huian's mission was. The level of commitment required didn't leave room for fluffy concepts like work/life balance. Huian's calling wasn't a hobbyist fascination with macramé. Technology was the only scalable tool available to help shape a better future. The question was whether people chose to participate in that future or not. Huian was a harbinger of that new reality. She would stop at nothing to push forward the inexorable, beautiful, conflicted locomotive of human civilization. Dystopias were the province of the undisciplined.

Unfortunately, success created its own problems. It made Cumulus a prime target for competitors, regulators, foreign governments, hackers, press, and activist investors. They'd grown too big not to become ensnarled in internal politics as well. Huian had to constantly question whether her executive team was working to advance the company or just their own careers. Sometimes it was difficult to tell whether so-called friends were interested in her or just her money. That's why she had agreed to create the Ghost Program with Graham, to separate allies from enemies and protect Cumulus's legacy. It was fucking hard. But fucking-hard problems were the only ones worth solving. History would be the judge.

Huian realized she was clenching her fists. Vera wanted more spontaneity? Inviting a trespassing photographer in for a drink was definitely a start. Not even Dr. Corvel could argue with that. Now all Huian had to do was figure out how to navigate Cumulus through turbulent seas and try to salvage her marriage at the same time.

"Ma'am?"

Huian shook her head, roping herself back from reverie.

"I've got Karl Dieter on the line."

Karl was the Cumulus VP who ran the Security division. He had been CEO of Security when Cumulus acquired it, and Huian had kept him on as the operating executive. Karl was gruff, efficient, and aggressive, which was probably why they got along well. His passion for vintage arcade games was beyond anything Huian had ever seen. Whenever they talked, she couldn't help but remember his basement lair that was packed to the brim with ancient pinball machines. Karl was consistent, but he didn't go beyond the call of duty like Graham did. He didn't think outside the box.

"Put him through," she said and heard the line switch over.

"Ma'am, we may have a situation," said Karl in his deep baritone. He wasn't one for small talk, another reason she liked him.

"What's up?" She rubbed her hands together slowly. Her palms were raw from spending hour after hour shooting last night. Tiny blisters were forming on the pads of her fingers. She hadn't played basketball for far too long.

"You told me to keep you in the loop about out-of-the-ordinary public safety situations."

"I remember."

"Well, to be honest, I'm not sure if this will amount to anything, but we have a crowd of a few hundred people marching up a street in West Oakland."

Huian frowned. "That's well outside the Green Zone."

"Correct, but we try to keep an eye on outbursts like this in order to deploy resources if we have to. If they reach the Fringe, we want to be ready."

"Why are they marching?"

"We actually don't know yet," said Karl. "Some kind of protest. I have people working on it."

Just what they needed, another spate of Slummer social activism. Vera would probably know what was going on, but Huian couldn't just call her and ask. No matter how hard Cumulus worked to build a better world, there were always people complaining. It was all well and good to point out other people's mistakes, but if you weren't actually going to step into the arena and present a viable alternative, you might as well just shut up. There were few people who frustrated Huian more than critics who produced nothing but hot air.

"Keep it under control," said Huian. "And let me know once you find out what it's all about."

"You got it, ma'am," said Karl.

She closed the connection and pulled up a feed on her office window. The protest was already all over the news. Bird's-eye view panoramics showed the group marching up the middle of Market Street in Oakland. Traffic was snarled, but Fleet's algorithms were rerouting around the disturbance.

Huian sighed. Sometimes, you just couldn't catch a break. Not that she was asking for one.

22

"I'M SORRY, MA'AM," said the detective. "But there's nothing else we can do at the moment."

Lilly's face puckered up in frustration. "How can that be? I just told you I saw the murderer leaving the scene."

The detective nodded, his face haggard. "You did, and I have all of that testimony recorded. Although the evidence you've provided is circumstantial, it will be taken into consideration. Thank you for coming forward. I or someone from the district attorney's office will likely be following up with you as the case moves forward."

Lilly didn't know what she had been expecting when she showed up at the Oakland Police Department, but it wasn't this. She had hoped to find a frenetic investigation in progress, with whiteboards covered in complex scribbles and someone standing in the middle taking charge of the situation. She looked around the room. The entire floor was deserted but for her and the weary detective. Empty desks and exposed air ducts were the only denizens. The faded beige carpet smelled of mildew.

"Where is everyone?"

The detective gave a defeated shrug. "Right now, most of our resources are deployed trying to keep the protest under control," he said. "But to be honest, it's pretty empty even on a good day. The city's been cutting our budget every year for the last decade, and the department's had no choice but to lay off many of our officers. I'd blame Mayor Gonzalez if I didn't know that it's happening to every other municipal department too."

"The protest?"

"You haven't heard? Almost seven hundred people are marching up Market Street. It's peaceful for the moment, but I'd recommend avoiding that area."

Lilly's stomach did a somersault. Her apartment was only a few blocks west of Market.

"Thanks, I'll keep well away," she said, recognizing it for a lie the minute the words came out of her mouth.

The detective nodded. He seemed about to say something but then held back.

"Good luck." He stood up and extended a hand.

She took his drift, shook the proffered hand, and headed for the door.

"Thanks," she said over her shoulder.

Back out on the street, she decided to walk. Her bike was locked up behind her apartment building. The Land Rover was still in Sara's driveway, BART didn't service her neighborhood, and the busses never ran on time, so she didn't have much of a choice. She would keep her eyes out for signs of the protest and skirt around it.

She worked her way northwest of downtown Oakland, deeper and deeper into the Slums. Early twentieth-century Edwardian houses had been converted into group homes. Laundry flapped from lines strung between the windows of monolithic concrete blocks of low-income housing. An intricate graffiti mural on a wide brick wall depicted the deeply lined face of a tired old woman. The portrait was powerfully evocative, and memories of Lilly's great aunt in the La Jolla nursing home rose from the dusty archives of her memory. Lilly reached for her camera before remembering she was out of film.

Pausing, she cocked her head to one side and pulled her phone from her pocket. That error message had been strange. She'd never had that issue before. She stepped down from the curb and snapped a few shots of the mural from various angles. The photos automatically uploaded to her Backend account without a hitch.

Well, at least on top of all of her other problems, she didn't need a new phone.

What she did need was a next move. The police had been a dead end. The file would likely be added to the stack of cold cases that piled up day after day. From what the detective had said, they weren't going to be making headway on Sara's murder anytime soon.

Lilly wasn't about to leave the investigation into her friend's killing to rot in red tape. She wasn't a Green Zone resident, so she couldn't go to Security for help. She could do her part, but Lilly knew she didn't have the skills or the resources to become a vigilante. Bruce Wayne had been a billionaire before he became Batman. The woman she had met the night before, Huian, had the means to help but not the motive. Lilly needed to find someone who cared as much as she did about finding the man she'd followed, and seeking justice for Sara's killing.

She almost tripped as she stepped off the next curb. Of course. It was blindingly obvious. She should have gone to him before the police anyway.

It took her another twenty minutes to make her way to the Compound.

23

TWO DOZEN PIT BULLS fought to break through the double-high chain-link fence topped in razor wire. Slobber flew from their mouths, and their lips retracted to display vicious sets of teeth as they jostled each other for the opportunity to eat Lilly alive. She hunched her shoulders and tried not to make eye contact as she walked along the sidewalk outside the fence. It surrounded an area the size of a city block with a massive warehouse in the middle. The dogs appeared to have free rein on the ring of bare asphalt around the building.

After what felt like forever, she reached the gate halfway down the block. The dogs followed close beside her on the inside of the fence the entire way, their barks echoing through the deserted street. Two enormous men with long dreadlocks stood in front of the gate, assault rifles dangling from straps on their shoulders. Although she'd heard many stories and rumors about the Compound at the heart of West Oakland, she'd never actually been here.

The men stared her down as she approached. One of them took a pull on a cigarette and the tip glowed orange. They didn't look like the kind of people used to accommodating casual visitors. She held her breath as she arrived in front of them.

"Quiet!" One yelled back at the dogs. To Lilly's amazement, they complied.

The other guy raised his face to the sky and blew out a cloud of smoke. "What do you want, girl?"

Lilly's palms were sweating. "I need to see Frederick."

"Hah." The men looked at each other and guffawed. "She *needs* to see Frederick. Maybe we should bring her a fresh coffee and donut while we're at it."

"I'm serious," said Lilly, forcing herself not to drop her eyes.

"Oho, she's *serious*."

The man dropped his cigarette to the pavement and ground it out with his heel. "Look, girl," he said. "Today is not a good day to see the boss. He's busy instigating insurrection. Come back in a week or two, and pitch whatever game you've got."

"Make that a month or two," said his friend, dreadlocks swirling as he shook his head.

"Yeah, a month or two. In the meantime, you can earn some brownie points by joining the protest."

"He'll want to see me," said Lilly, trying not to let her frustration bleed into her voice.

"Boss knows his own mind and his own wants. We don't get paid to prognosticate that shit."

Lilly steeled herself.

"I know who killed Sara Levine," she said.

They both tensed.

"What did you just say?"

"I said, I know who killed Sara Levine."

The glance they exchanged conveyed no humor this time. One stepped away, unclipped a walkie-talkie from his belt, and started talking into it.

"You better not be fucking around," said the other. "Or things are about to go very badly for you."

"You think I don't know that?"

The guy just shrugged.

A minute later, his partner returned.

"Come with me," he said. "And give me your hand." He extended his own, not for a handshake but like someone offering to hold the hand of a sweetheart.

"My hand?"

"The dogs," he said. "So they know you're a friend."

"Sit!" yelled the other guard. The pit bulls all lowered onto their haunches in unison. He proceeded to enter a code and the gate slid open.

The guard holding Lilly's hand led her through. As soon as the gate closed behind them, the dogs came up and sniffed at her. One licked her forearm with a wide, rough tongue.

"They like women." His tone had lost its edge.

Lilly looked up at the huge building they were walking toward. Brightly colored murals covered walls that stretched hundreds of meters in both directions. She recognized some of the scenes from history textbooks. Malcolm X stared out through his signature circular glasses. Aung San Suu Kyi spoke into a microphone in profile. Bandoliers of ammunition crisscrossed Pancho Villa's chest. A black-and-white feather rose from behind the head of Sitting Bull. A bloody ice ax hung from Mara Winkel's hand. Lee Kuan Yew waved to an expectant crowd. Along the bottom of the walls, stylized Oakland trees rose as if growing from fertile blacktop.

The dogs hung back as they approached the entrance. A corrugated metal door slid open and closed behind them as they stepped inside.

The interior of the building was a vast open space segmented into sections by waist-high partitions. The sections varied in size and shape, and were connected by walkways that wove the entire building into an intricate puzzle. But Lilly realized this later. The overwhelming first impression was of prolific activity.

People were everywhere, doing everything. Workers in masks and gloves separated and bagged a white mountain of cocaine in the middle of a wide table. A group of teenagers sweated through a workout routine as an instructor barked out instructions. A small army of people typed away at keyboards in front of large computer displays. Heavily muscled laborers piled crates into trucks in the loading dock at the far end. Analysts argued in front of whiteboards covered in diagrams and scribbles. Cooks tended a pit barbecue the size of a bus with a complex system of air ducts venting through the ceiling. Three fighters sparred in a mixed martial arts ring. An early 1990s De La Soul album played at low volume over a unified speaker system that connected the entire space.

"Holy shit," Lilly said under her breath. Nobody gave her a second glance.

"That about covers it," said her escort, and Lilly thought she could detect an undercurrent of pride in his tone.

They made their way through the maze to a relatively quiet far corner. Unlike the other sections, this one had full walls and a ceiling so it looked like a box inside the larger space. The guard rapped his knuckles on the door.

"Send her in," said a muffled voice from inside.

Her escort gave her a mock salute. "I really hope you've got something for him." Then he turned away and walked off into the mayhem.

Lilly opened the door and stepped through. Beyond was a large sunken conference room. A table filled much of the space in the middle, chairs scattered around it. From inside, Lilly could see that the walls of the room were actually windows of adjustable opacity, currently displaying various dashboards, graphs, and video feeds.

Three people looked up at her from where they stood around the table. A middle-aged woman in a denim jumpsuit chewed on the end of a pencil. Tattoos covered every inch of the exposed arms of a thickly muscled younger guy with dreadlocks in the same style as the gate guards. And then there was Frederick. He was a tall, slender, aristocratic black man in his mid-fifties with short-cropped gray hair and the physique of a former athlete. He wore his trademark immaculate tuxedo.

"Can you give us the room?" Frederick's voice was sonorous but surprisingly soft.

The woman looked like she was about to object, but then she and the dreadlocked man filed out the same door Lilly had entered through.

Lilly stepped down into the sunken area around the table. Frederick looked her up and down. Up close, she could see that his eyes were red-rimmed.

"Lilly Miyamoto," he said. This was the second time in twenty-four hours that a stranger had cited her full name before they had been introduced. "Sara mentioned you a number of times. Among other things, she said you were the only one keeping her beloved Land Rover alive after all these years."

Lilly remembered oil-soaked afternoons spent under the truck. "It's a fine vehicle," she said. "They built them to last and meant it."

"Indeed. Sometimes I wonder whether I was built to last."

Frederick eyed her for a long moment. Then he pressed his fingertips onto the table in front of him, forming a little cathedral of open space under each hand. His sigh was laced with pain.

"Duncan tells me," he said, "that you have information pertaining to Sara's murder. Specifically, that you claim to know the identity of the perpetrator."

"I don't know his name, and I didn't see him shoot her," said Lilly. "But when I arrived this morning to return the car, I saw him leaving through the back gate and followed him." She lifted the camera from where it hung on its strap.

"And I have pictures."

24

"LILLY, MEET HENOK ADDISU, our resident public relations guru."

Frederick nodded to a handsome spectacled man in front of a triptych of widescreen monitors. They were standing in a small section of the larger warehouse space that was immediately adjacent to Frederick's closed conference room. "Before joining the team here, Henok was an investigative reporter, wrote a very popular blog, and did a whole bunch of other things I still don't fully understand. Needless to say, he's become an integral part of our little family. He is leading the, ah, intellectual side of our internal investigation into this morning's homicide."

Henok stood and shook Lilly's hand.

"Lilly," said Frederick, "is a photojournalist with key evidence relating to the case. I trust you will put your minds together and help figure out this mess."

"I'm just a wedding photographer, really," said Lilly.

Frederick raised an eyebrow. "That's not how Sara described you, and I never knew her to be wrong about reading people."

Lilly shrugged and tried to hide the pride and pain that rose within her.

"Wait a minute," she said. "You do public relations?"

Frederick laid a hand on Henok's shoulder. "All organizations are media organizations now," said the younger man. "Nobody can afford not to consider what to say or how to say it. Your story defines your identity."

"I don't know media," said Frederick, "but I know politics. And the former can make quite an impact on the latter."

Lilly frowned. "What does any of this have to do with Sara?"

"We have reason to suspect that Sara's murder may have been politically motivated," said Frederick, something flashing behind his eyes. "And I believe in fighting fire with fire." He nodded, as if something had been decided. "Well then, I will let you two get down to business. Lilly, I have already made a deposit to your account to cover any incidental expenses related to the investigation. If you require any additional resources, let me or Henok know immediately. With your help, justice will be served. Now, please excuse me. There is unrest to foment."

Frederick adjusted his tuxedo jacket, turned away, and disappeared back into the conference center. Had he just deputized her?

Henok stared after him. "I've never seen him like that," he said.

"Like what?" asked Lilly.

Henok shook his head slowly. "So emotional," he said. "Sara must have meant a lot to him. I mean, she was obviously a legal adviser to him and they were, well, together. But still…"

Lilly didn't know how to respond. Frederick had appeared supremely calm to her. Only the red around his eyes had hinted at the pain he must be feeling at the loss of his lover. Then again, this was the first time she'd met him. Maybe he wasn't an easy man to read.

"Here." Henok snipped off a tiny piece of duct tape from a roll on his desk.

"What's this?" asked Lilly.

"Security precaution," said Henok. "Paste it on your phone's camera when you're not using it. You never know who might be watching." He held up his phone to display how it was done and then handed her a small plastic clip attached to a foam earplug. "This fits snugly over the microphone to muffle audio." He shrugged.

Lilly obliged. "What did Frederick mean about the murder being politically motivated?"

Henok waved her over to his screens. "Check it out."

Lilly walked around the desk and shuddered at what she saw. Ultra-high-definition images were scattered across all three displays in a complex mosaic. They had photographed every inch of Sara's house and yard from every possible angle. Hundreds of images of the scene in the living room cycled through. They had even surveyed the inside of the Land Rover and pulled the latest satellite shots of the roof. Every object and detail was digitally tagged to notations in a separate window.

"The police collected all the evidence," he said, "but Frederick talked to the detectives and we did a first pass before their forensics guys messed everything up. We don't have any of the physical stuff, but we've logged everything digitally in pretty much every possible way."

Lilly tried to suppress a sudden onset of nausea. She couldn't believe she had parked the Land Rover in Sara's driveway only this morning. The most pressing thing on her mind had been how to tell her friend about her misadventures. That seemed like some parallel universe now, a different person living a different life.

"This is where it gets interesting," Henok said, indicating a grid of pictures of individual sheets of paper covered in text, some splattered with brownish dried blood. Lilly remembered the piles of paperwork on the coffee table in front of Sara's body.

"Sara was working on a class-action lawsuit targeting Cumulus," said Henok. "We knew that already. What we didn't know was how good her case was. Frederick has another attorney going through everything line by line. But it's clear that she had acquired damning evidence from a few disgruntled employees that would have put the company directly into the line of fire from SEC, IRS, and Justice. It would throw Wall Street into chaos. Given how much infrastructure Cumulus controls, it would be disruptive even at a local level. Plus, the PR fallout would be massive."

Lilly tried to rein in her thoughts and bring herself back to the present. "So you think that Cumulus murdered her?" It seemed like a very, very long shot. It was a little too far-fetched to imagine a Silicon Valley tech company ordering an assassination. That was the stuff of conspiracy forums.

Henok gave her a sidelong glance, picking up on her tone. "We have no direct evidence of that," he said, a little defensively. "But if you don't know who's responsible for the course of action, it's good to start by identifying who has the most to gain from the results. Sara's case relied on sources she hadn't yet revealed. Her lawsuit died with her."

"But what about Occam's razor?" said Lilly. "It could have been a robbery gone wrong, or an ex, or someone she previously prosecuted getting revenge, or an attempted rape, or maybe a nut got his hands on his first Glock and wanted to see if it worked."

"Nothing was stolen, she wasn't raped, and Frederick has people looking into her personal and professional background to filter for potential enemies," said Henok. "But there's no way we wouldn't know if someone local did this. It wasn't our guys. And our guys control those corners. That means this asshole wasn't from Oakland. And if that's true, then it was probably targeted."

Lilly tapped her camera. "I've got shots of the asshole in question right here."

Henok's eyes widened. "Well, holy shit. What are you waiting for?" He held out a USB jack.

She shook her head. "It's analog," she said. "I need to develop them in my darkroom."

"Seriously? I didn't even realize they still made film."

"You just have to know where to look."

"How long will it take you to develop them?"

"I can do it this afternoon."

"Good." He pulled up a window filled with text. "I'm working up a blog post about the murder, and I want those shots."

"A blog post? Why?"

"*Why* is Frederick's department. I'm more of a *what* and *how* guy," he said. "But if I were to hazard a guess, I'd imagine it has to do with grassroots populism. The protest and all that jazz."

Since she'd entered this building, Lilly had felt like she was running three steps behind. "I've had one hell of a day," she said. "So humor me and start at the beginning."

Henok looked up. "I'll make you a deal," he said, adjusting his glasses. "You get me those photos and I'll catch you up."

25 ▬▬▬

"JESUS FUCKING CHRIST!" Martín stumbled backward and fell into a sitting position on the carpeted floor.

Graham smiled. It was almost too easy. It was incredible how much routine governed people's lives. The truly miraculous part was that criminals didn't take even more advantage of it than they already did.

Every single night Martín ate a late dinner with his wife and his twin boys, and then came out into the separate studio office in the backyard to catch up on whatever work he hadn't been able to get done at the Tectonix office that day. Every single night. And with root access to the Cumulus network, Graham could simply scan back through time to see the records of his geolocation and recordings from every sensor on his phone and any networked device within range. Given that most devices were connected to Cumulus in one way or another, it gave him a godlike view of the entire history of pretty much anyone or anything he wanted to see. Even better, the Ghost Program rendered him digitally invisible to Cumulus's ecosystem. His presence was automatically wiped clean from the system that recorded every-one else and that Security and law enforcement relied on. It was the ultimate operational carte blanche. Agency analysts could kiss his ass.

"No need to get upset, Martín." Graham spun around in the office chair to face him. "I'm just here for a casual chat between friends."

Martín pushed himself back a few meters like a crab and then rose to his feet.

"What the fuck are you doing in my house?" His pupils dilated.

"Well," said Graham. "If we want to get technical, this is your office." He raised his hands in mock concession. "But to address the spirit of your question, certainly we're on good enough terms that you'd be more than happy to invite me into your home?"

"Good terms? Are you out of your goddamn mind?" He made a visible effort to get his breathing under control. He extended a hand to the wall to keep his balance.

"Oh, I can assure you that I am entirely sane," said Graham. "But I appreciate your concern for my mental well-being."

Martín's Adam's apple bobbed up and down as he swallowed. "Get the hell off of my property or I'm going to call Security."

Graham raised his eyebrows. "So soon? But we have much to discuss."

"We have *nothing* to discuss. I did everything you asked. I betrayed my team, my shareholders, and myself and turned down Huian's outrageously rich acquisition offer for no good reason. Our deal is over. Done. Kaput." Martín sliced the air with his hand to emphasize the point.

Graham smiled wanly. "Martín, Martín, Martín," he said. "If only it were that simple. But our deal is very far from over. Really, you should be looking at this as the beginning of a long and fruitful partnership." Graham nodded as if he had convinced himself of the argument's veracity. "Yes, and a profitable one too. Why, just by your gracious accommodation of my request to turn them down, Cumulus doubled its acquisition offer. I'd say that has to be worth something. In fact, you should be thanking me."

Muscles worked in Martín's jaw. "The day I thank you for blackmailing me will be the day I kill you with my bare hands."

"Let's hope it doesn't come to that," said Graham. "In the meantime, I think you will be quite keen on our next little collaboration."

Martín just stared daggers at him.

"I can't pretend to be an expert on technology companies," said Graham. "But when I decided to make my foray into Silicon Valley, I did my best to learn the basics and read about the history of the industry. Jeff Bezos, the founder and former chief executive of Amazon, famously opined that people who were right a lot of the time were also people who often changed their minds. Strong views, weakly held. He valued flexibility over consistency of thought. He knew that the smartest people can accommodate contradiction and constantly challenge and refine their own point of view."

"Get to the fucking point." Martín pressed his lips together into a thin line. "If you're going to manipulate me, don't try to do it with philosophy."

Graham sighed. It was always so disappointing to work with someone who didn't appreciate the finer details. You just couldn't win them all.

"You will reach out to Huian," said Graham. "And tell her that you have reconsidered her offer and have decided to accept. You will sell Tectonix to Cumulus."

All the color drained from Martín's face. He stood mute for a full minute.

"But the board," he said. "I've spent every ounce of my reputation convincing them to back my vision and turn down the acquisition. I can't just come back the next day and reverse the decision. It won't make sense. It would be too much of a red flag. They'll refuse. They'll find a way to throw me out."

Graham's expression hardened. "Then I suggest you get creative."

"It's impossible."

"Necessity is the mother of invention. And neither of us want that video of Stephanie being double-teamed to reach the prying eyes of the internet." Martín's eldest daughter was studying particle physics at Princeton, and had developed a propensity for threesomes. In her latest foray, she had inadvertently left her phone on the dresser where its camera had a perfect angle on her giving one track runner a blowjob while another one took her from behind. She hadn't been actively recording, but Cumulus had persistent records from every sensor on every device. Graham's access had allowed him to simply pull whatever records he wanted. "It's just harmless experimentation, but some people can be so close-minded and unforgiving."

Martín charged, fists swinging in wild arcs. Graham ducked under the flurry of blows and drove a shoulder into Martín's solar plexus. Then he swept Martín's feet out from under him and twisted an arm behind the man's back as he fell. By the time Martín hit the floor, Graham had the arm torqued into a bind.

With this little visit, Graham's initial gambit was nearly complete. The pieces had been set in motion. Cumulus was arguably the most powerful organization in the world, on par with national governments. He had installed himself as its intelligence chief, and proved his worth to Huian. But he wanted to wield power, not simply do the bidding of the powerful. That meant reversing his relationship with Huian. Oh, he had no desire to be CEO. Official leaders were nominal figureheads at best, distracting from the players who really pulled the strings. He had already used the powers she had initially granted him to isolate her and enflame her paranoia. She depended on him more and more for trusted advice. By controlling her reality, he could deliver precisely timed fear, hope, and insight. Huian was his marionette, and he would rule Cumulus through her. He held her in a bind tighter than the one securing this man's arm.

Martín gasped like a dying fish. The air had been knocked out of him by the impact.

Graham leaned down and whispered into his ear. "I'm sure a promising young woman like her would be able to get out from under it. Eventually."

It *was* too easy.

26

EMPLOYEES CRUISED ALONG the network of internal campus paths on skateboards. Despite the chill in the breeze coming in from under the Golden Gate Bridge, a group was holding an impromptu beach volleyball tournament on a grid of courts. But now that autumn was in full swing, sweaters and boots were everywhere.

As Cumulus had grown, Huian had noticed how the apparel had changed. There was obviously no dress code, and in the company's early days, their small team of developers had not been unfashionable so much as intentionally flouting any norm that didn't suit their personal comfort. Hoodies and science-fiction-themed T-shirts ruled the day. But as they grew from an uppity startup into a Silicon Valley behemoth, Cumulus had needed to hire marketers, analysts, salespeople, strategists, attorneys, managers, and many, many others to fill in all the operational niches an organization of their size required. This new influx of people shifted the overall culture of the place, and now the atmosphere was trendier. Hand-cut leather, designer clothes that tried very hard not to look like designer clothes, and expedition-grade outdoor gear were the new norm. The geeks had given way to the hipsters.

Huian entered the squat gray building that was Security's head-quarters. She passed through a series of biometric scanners and other sensor equipment, and then descended three floors and entered the Security command center. Screens covered the walls of the large circular room showing views of a variety of ongoing crises from all over the world. Analysts worked in groups, their screens covered in code and complex interfaces. There was a raised dais in the middle of the room with a wide table and a dozen chairs.

Karl sat at one end of the table, deep in conversation with two of his lieutenants. An analyst approached the trio, gave a report, and returned to his station with new orders. A constant buzz of energy and activity gave the command center the atmosphere of a beehive.

Huian walked up to the dais and caught Karl's eye. He waved the lieutenants away.

"I came to check up on the protest situation," she said.

"I figured as much," said Karl. "That's why I'm down here too."

He waved to an analyst, and the surrounding screens resolved into a panoply of live video feeds.

Karl gestured. "You're seeing shots from our eye-in-the-sky sur-veillance drones, Bandwidth Wi-Fi drones, delivery drones, Fleet vehicles, security cameras, and phones that have good angles." He waved his hand at an adjacent display that was cycling through text far too fast to read and flagging specific words with highlights. "We're running a full semantic model on any communication coming in or out of the group, audio, text, or passive recording from phones in people's pockets. Same thing for all the news feeds. That should help monitor the overall temperament of the group and alert us in advance if they enter a downward spiral. Fleet is using its swarm algorithm to route around it. We certainly don't want an accident."

The group on-screen had swelled from hundreds to a few thou-sand, stretching over a few city blocks as they marched. Huian had always found social dynamics to be a fascinating subject. People talked about internet products and media going viral. But just like any biomimetic concept, the viral growth of ideas closely mirrored the actual epidemiology of real world viruses. And ideas had gone viral long before the internet was invented. Mob mentality. Religious zeal. Anything that enabled groupthink.

"As you can see, they're still far from the Green Zone and out of our area of interest," said Karl. "But I have a pod tracking it just in case that changes."

"What about local police?"

Karl waved a hand, and one of the cameras zoomed in, showing a few uniformed officers walking ahead of and behind the crowd.

"They have a small presence," said Karl. "Mostly just preventative. They're hoping that seeing cops will prevent people from doing anything stupid. Our liaison checked in with the chief. Oakland has only one riot unit now. They're prepped, but I doubt they'll bring them out unless it gets really ugly."

She and Karl had stood at this very table and watched conflicts break out all over the world. Sometimes the Department of Defense would send a representative to use Cumulus assets to complement the federal surveillance network and monitor an ongoing operation. But it was rare to watch something happening so close to home. Although the crowd was still in the middle of the Slums, it wasn't that far from her house up in the hills. Maybe a twenty-minute Fleet ride.

"Have you made any progress figuring out why this started in the first place?"

Karl grimaced. "It's always hard to give a concrete answer to a question like that when we're in the middle of a developing situation. But it appears that a local resident was murdered in her home this morning. She was shot multiple times, and it looks like it was targeted. Police are currently in the middle of forensics, but they don't have any strong leads so far."

Huian frowned. "What's the annual homicide rate in the Oakland Slums?"

"Two hundred and seventy-nine last year."

"At risk of sounding callous, what's so special about this one? There weren't two hundred and seventy-nine protests last year."

"In this case, the victim was respected and well-liked by local residents. Hopefully, we'll find out more once the investigation gets moving, but I doubt it. These days, OPD murder investigations essentially amount to adding a new file to the pile of cold cases." Karl shrugged. "Your question is good, but not easy to answer. First, because we don't yet know enough. Second, because these kinds of things often don't have clear-cut logic behind them. Often, resentment or frustration builds up over time, and then something small instigates an explosion."

Huian thought about her various fights with Vera over the years.

"I totally understand," she said. She made a mental note to talk to Graham. She could use his counsel on this.

27

LILLY DIDN'T REALIZE she was crying until she reached up to wipe the wetness from her cheeks.

The photos were hanging in her bathroom-turned-darkroom. While she waited for them to dry, she had wrapped herself up in a fleece blanket and collapsed onto the couch. Now that she was home, the tides of adrenaline that had surged through her body all day long were finally receding. Exhaustion followed close in their wake.

The world had gone haywire. Just twenty-four hours ago, she had been finishing up at the wedding and quietly resenting Marian's managerial style. Since then, she had escaped a narrow run-in with Security thanks to a cryptic billionaire, discovered Sara's corpse and shadowed her murderer, and been enlisted by the bereaved Godfather of Oakland to assist in the unofficial effort to avenge his dead lover. A few tears were probably healthy.

She burrowed deeper into the couch. It was a relief to be back in the tiny apartment she called home. Her kitchenette was stocked with instant noodles. The sofa was lumpy but comforting in its familiarity. The oak coffee table reminded her of the smell of sweat and sawdust. Her dad had used the project to teach her a thing or two about wood-working. She had loved the rough warmth of his hand over hers as he showed her how to use the lathe. The sheen of the varnish gleamed in her memory.

She jerked up into a sitting position. She must have drifted off. Her phone was ringing. She snatched it up.

"Hello?"

"Are they ready? I really need to get this story out. Frederick is breathing down my neck."

Because her mind was still scrambling back toward consciousness, it took her a moment to recognize the voice. Henok. It was Henok. So he was asking about the pictures. Lilly noticed how dark her apartment was. Hadn't afternoon light been shining on the coffee table when she sat down on the couch?

"What time is it?" she asked, trying to keep the grogginess out of her voice.

"Eight," said Henok. "I thought it wasn't supposed to take that long. Seriously, I don't understand why you don't just shoot digital."

Shit. The pictures would have been ready ages ago. She must have slept for hours. Pinching the bridge of her nose, she tried to get her thoughts in order.

"I'll be right over with them," she said.

"Good, see you soon."

Henok was one of those people who quickly settled into familiar ease with new acquaintances. Lilly had a small group of very close friends. Henok seemed like the kind of guy who befriended anyone he met. That kind of easy trust required more emotional generosity than Lilly could usually manage, but she found the trait endearing. That said, she didn't know how to feel about the whole Frederick situation. It was well known that he ran the Oakland Slums' organized-crime ring. Visiting his headquarters had made it even more blatant. But if he was that out-in-the-open about it, he must have some understanding with the police. And the police themselves hadn't appeared too keen on doing much of anything about Sara's murder. To Lilly, Frederick's enforcers weren't much different from Security officers. Both carried the threat of violence against those too poor or weak to afford protection or defend themselves. And, to Frederick's credit, he *was* trying to investigate Sara's murder. Vigilante justice it might be, but if the alternative was inaction, then maybe he was on to something.

Walking over to the kitchen sink, she splashed some cold water on her face. Then she pulled a manila envelope out of a drawer, and went to collect the pictures.

Three years ago, she had spent a week converting her bathroom into a darkroom. Duct tape secured double layers of black garbage bag over the small window. She had replaced the standard light with a red bulb that didn't ruin the photo paper. Towels were stuffed into place around every edge of the door, and then taped over. For the photos to develop properly, she couldn't afford to let just any old photons in. Lines of string connected the shower rod to nails she'd hammered into the opposite wall. The newly developed photos hung like laundry.

Now that she had opened the bathroom door, the normal light from the living room mixed with the glow from the darkroom's bulb to bathe the pictures in an ominous amber, diminishing color and contrast. Sara's body lay splayed in her living room. A figure hurried away from her house via the side gate. The man ducked into the West Oakland BART Station. He entered the North Berkeley café, and exited in different clothes. His face turned over his shoulder to check out the ass of the passing jogger. He exited the small office building housing the private practice of Dr. Flint Corvel.

I apologize if this is a little forward. But I think you've got a killer sense of style. Lilly shivered despite herself. It was hard to believe she had been so close to him. She had wanted more than anything to disappear, terrified that he'd hear her pounding heart. But the waiting Fleet had whisked him away.

She shook herself. Henok needed these. She reached up and released each photo from the clips securing it to the string, carefully sliding each one into the manila envelope. Her little darkroom was an incongruous place for these graphic images. Its tubs, strings, and chemical baths were more accustomed to smiling bridal parties.

As she sealed the envelope, she considered the irony of her professional ambitions made real. For years, she had been saving to finance her dream of covering foreign conflicts. Violence abroad seemed somehow exotic. Correspondents could approach close enough to take a picture while still remaining emotionally apart. Now, Frederick was financing her to cover a conflict that was far too close to home.

In her many daydreams, she had never flinched from doing what needed doing, no matter the circumstances.

The Fleet delivered her to the Compound in less than ten minutes. On her way home earlier that day, she had checked her account to discover that Frederick had transferred in $25,000 to cover expenses. That was more money than she had ever made on a project. Hell, that was almost as much money as she made a year. So she took a Fleet instead of risking getting mugged while riding her bike at night. It wasn't worth losing the pictures.

The guards waved her in without hassle. The dogs recognized her scent this time, and she walked from the gate to the door sans escort. Floodlights illuminated the streets and sidewalks around the warehouse, but left the building in shadow. The pit bulls shouldered each other out of the way to sniff and lick at her hands. She ruffled the fur on the head of the one that was smaller and somehow sadder than the others.

Even though it was late in the evening, the interior of the Compound still hummed with activity. The soundtrack had transitioned to blues. Lilly wound her way back through the maze of subsections to find Henok. The glow of his monitors set his face awash in blue. He had on a big pair of headphones, and was completely absorbed in his work. She walked around behind him and saw a simple text document on the center display with web mock-ups previewing the final version in various formats on the side displays.

He twitched when she tapped him on the shoulder. He peeled off the headphones, and she could hear a peal of thunder emanate from them.

"You some kind of ninja?" he asked. "I almost peed my pants."

"What are you listening to?"

He smiled sheepishly. "I actually don't like music." He waved a hand to indicate the harmonica solo on the building's speaker system. "It distracts me. So I listen to nature sounds to drown it out." He raised his eyebrows. "You have 'em?"

She nodded and pulled the manila envelope from her jacket, handing it to him.

He accepted it and opened the seal carefully, almost reverently. Clearing a space on the desk, he removed each twenty-eight-by-thirty-six-centimeter photo, and arranged them in a grid. Lilly watched curiously as he stood and leaned close to inspect every individual shot. Then he stepped back and looked at the grid from afar. Returning to the table, he started rearranging the photos into various orders and combinations. Occasionally, he'd cock his head to the side and squint at them, mumbling to himself. Then he would shuffle them again. He went through a few iterations.

Finally, he rapped his knuckles on the table and let out a long low whistle.

"Sara was right," he said turning to appraise Lilly. "Your talent is wasted on weddings. I've worked with many photojournalists over the years, and these shots are Pulitzer-quality."

Lilly was taken aback. Then she recovered enough to realize he must be messing with her. "Screw you," she said, anger rising. "It's not like I had time to set up the composition. I was scared shitless and trying to get angles on the guy's face, not building a portfolio."

A confused expression flashed across Henok's face and then settled into something sterner than she had yet seen. "I'm serious," he said. "These are incredibly powerful pictures. They will make a splash. And I've worked in media for long enough to know not to try to predict stuff like that."

A blush rose to Lilly's cheeks, and words failed her. The anger faded, and despite everything, pride stirred within her. Nobody had ever said anything like that about her work.

"Alright," said Henok, all enthusiasm now. "Let's scan these bad boys and take the world by storm."

He scooped up the photos, and dashed over to a corner of his work area to feed them into the scanner.

Meanwhile, Lilly put her hands on the back of his chair and peered at the screen. This was the story Henok had been working on all day. It was long, and would probably take a half hour to read in full. Right away, the narrative gripped her. The first sentence drew her in, and the first paragraph hooked her completely. Henok was good at his job.

The article wove various threads together. Sara's personal and professional history. Her various high-profile cases targeting corporate bad actors and government corruption. Her pro bono work defending Slummers, and her long involvement in the West Oakland community. A condensed history of poverty and crisis in the Slums juxtaposed against the urban segregation and private social services in the Green Zone. The flimsy details of the case, and the sorely lacking efforts of local law enforcement. The improbability of traditional motives and local suspects. The burgeoning protest congregating on the streets.

"Damnit," said Henok over by the scanner. "What the hell is wrong with this thing?"

The question sounded rhetorical, so Lilly ignored him and returned to the story. Details from the case Sara had been building against Cumulus and the existential threat it might have posed to the company. The history of Cumulus, its sometimes predatory legal tactics, the appeal of its promise, and the sad reality for people not able to pay for inclusion in its service bundle.

Lilly's knuckles whitened as she gripped the back of the chair. What had she just read? She scanned back through the paragraph, confusion and disbelief making her doubt herself. But it was there, just as she had thought. Huian Li. The article described how she had founded Cumulus two decades before and built it into the tech giant it was today. It told the story of her Chinese Indonesian parents fleeing Jakarta when a local political faction moved against their family and how they had raised their daughter in Palo Alto. It even described her passion for basketball.

Lilly tried to control her breathing. There couldn't be that many women named Huian with mansions in the Bay Area. Fewer still who might build a subterranean basketball court into their basement. Those intense eyes stared down Lilly through the veil of memory. *Uncuff her or I'll have your damn badge.* No wonder those Security thugs had obeyed her. She was their boss's boss's boss's boss.

Lilly snatched up her phone and did an image search for Huian Li. Sure enough, there was the woman from the night before. But instead of a sweat-stained oversized T-shirt, she was dressed in impeccable business attire, and speaking to a room full of reporters. There she was again on the front page of *Wired*. Scrolling down, Lilly saw she had been featured by most major publications numerous times. She was the archetypal techno-industrialist. *You don't know?* That's how Huian had responded when Lilly asked her name. Then that shadow of a smile had flashed across her face. *I'm Huian. Pleased to meet you.* The CEO of Cumulus had mixed her a damn cocktail, and Lilly hadn't even realized it.

"Out of the way." Henok nudged her aside. "Something's wrong with the stupid scanner. I got the photo of the crime scene, but then it stopped working once I tried to do the ones of the perp. Next time, use a digital camera, okay? That way we can skip these shenanigans."

Lilly tried to recover her composure while Henok played with various settings on the screen.

"You'd think that people would have figured out by now how to make these things just work like they're supposed to," said Henok, frustration brimming in his tone. "Scanners, teleconference systems— why does the simplest shit always break first?"

She made a noncommittal grunt, supporting his assessment of technology's tendency to fail right when you needed it most. Internally, she was still trying to parse her new discovery. She had trespassed on the property of Cumulus's founder just to take a few sunset pictures. It was damn lucky Huian had taken pity on her. If those Security guys had driven off with her in the back of one of their SUVs, she probably would have ended up in a ditch.

Henok growled. "This thing is broken," he said.

"Don't you guys have other scanners?"

"We do," he said. "But they're halfway across the building in the hacker section." Getting up from his chair, he collected the photos that had failed to scan and started off along a pathway.

"Come on," he said, looking back over his shoulder. She followed.

The hacker section was a jungle of widescreen displays, bundles of brightly colored cables, and scattered pieces of electronic debris. It was much bigger than the area where Henok worked—almost twenty people sat writing code, monitoring releases, and reviewing patches.

"This is quite an operation," said Lilly.

"Software is just as important for us as for any other kind of organization," said Henok. "It's become a core competency by necessity."

They found three scanners lined up on a small table in the corner. They didn't look like they got much use. Henok fed in the photos and initiated the scan, keying it to save the results to his account. The scan completed.

"Alright," he said, pulling up his account to check the file on his phone. "Second time's the—shit!" He face contorted in frustration. "What the fuck? This one's not working either. It just throws up an error message."

He moved on to the next scanner. Same result. Then the final scanner. Same result.

A vivid memory flashed through Lilly's mind. A tired old woman's face staring out from a brick wall.

"Try your phone," she said. It was still nascent but there was definitely something wrong here.

"Huh?"

"Try your phone. Just use the camera to take an image of the physical photo, and you can upload that to your blog."

Henok frowned but seemed to concede that this might work. He whipped a phone from his pocket, peeled the duct tape off the camera, lined up the picture of the man looking over his shoulder at the retreating jogger, and took a picture. Lilly held her breath.

"God*damn*it," he said. "Now my phone isn't working either."

An idea was unfurling in her mind. "Do you have a wallet on you?"

He looked up, confused. "Sure," he said.

"Give it to me." She held out a hand.

"So you're going to remedy the situation by robbing me blind." But his tone was self-consciously petulant. He placed a worn leather wallet in her hand.

She removed his ID and placed it on the first scanner. "Is this still set up to save to your account?"

"Yeah, I haven't reset it yet," he said. "But it doesn't work. What are you trying to do?"

She ran the scan.

"Did it work?"

He made a face like he was indulging a small child. But then his expression crumbled into confusion. "What the hell?"

"Did it work or not?"

"Yeah, it saved no problem. No error."

She replaced the photo of the man and ran a scan.

"Did it work?"

He frowned. "Nope."

"Give me the phone."

He handed it over. She snapped a picture of the license.

"No error," she reported.

Then she snapped a picture of the photo of the man.

"Error." She looked up at Henok and found him staring back at her. "When I was following him, I ran out of film," she said. "Naturally, I tried with my phone, but I got the same error message and the pictures I took wouldn't save. When I tried the phone camera later on something else, it worked fine."

His eyes seemed to focus on a point a thousand miles away.

"Something is deeply, deeply fucked," he said.

"I am inclined to agree."

28

HUIAN TOWELED OFF HER HAIR. Steam rose from her naked skin. She liked her showers scalding. She had worked late, and ultimately decided to spend the night at the office. Cumulus headquarters was designed with such eventualities in mind. A private bedroom with full bathroom abutted her office. Freshly pressed clothes hung ready for her in the closet.

As CEO, she was in a permanent state of catch-up. There were always a dozen things that required her attention. No matter how effectively she delegated, new problems emerged. The faster they grew, the thornier the problems became. Lately, she had begun to doubt some of the members of her executive team. Graham had even let her know that Karl had been quietly approached with other job offers. He hadn't yet accepted any, of course. But it forced Huian to consider how fleeting the world could be. One day, you had the best team in the world. The next, they might scatter like so many dandelion seeds. One day, you were married. The next, your spouse left you. Richard had been the latest to go, but he wouldn't be the last.

Tossing the towel to the floor, she examined herself in the mirror. Streaks of white and gray peppered her jet-black hair. Lines creased at the corners of her eyes. Her breasts were less firm than they once were, her muscles less defined. But despite all that, she knew she looked good for her age. Not as good as that young photographer, but still in the running.

Certainly, Huian was busy. The nature of her job leeched the meaning out of that word. But if she was truly honest with herself, that wasn't the reason she hadn't gone home last night.

She slithered into her underwear and donned slacks, blouse, and blazer. No. She hadn't wanted to go home. Right now, home meant Vera. And Vera meant loss. Whether or not they might reconcile, Huian knew it would never be the same. There were certain things that were irrevocable. You might turn a new page, but you couldn't backtrack.

Standing at the vanity, she paused before starting to apply makeup. Not today. She replaced the cosmetics, unused. There were times when appearances mattered, and there were times when you just had to be real.

She stepped out into her office and pulled the hidden door to the private bedroom shut. A tray sat on her desk with a bagel smothered in cream cheese and lox, a glass of fresh-squeezed orange juice, and a velvety cappuccino. A handwritten note from Tom wished her good morning with a little smiley face.

The bagel was delicious, the flavors perfectly complemented by a sprinkling of capers and pepper. As she munched on her breakfast, she gazed out the window of her office. Intermittent clouds passed before the morning sun, softening the light shining on her fair city. The bay was calm and glassy. Cumulus employees wandered the campus pathways, getting ready to start their day. Remembering enjoying the same view yesterday afternoon, she was struck by how impervious the world was to the vagaries of human drama. People's successes and failures, lives and deaths, were as nothing to the universe they inhabited. Just flickers in the ether. You had only one chance to make your mark.

"Ma'am?" Tom's voice came over the sound system.

"Yes, Tom? Thank you for breakfast, by the way. It's heavenly."

"Of course, ma'am, my pleasure."

"So, what's up?"

"Ma'am, Karl asked to see you as soon as you were available. You needed the sleep so I didn't wake you. But now that you've eaten, I figured you'd want to know."

The best executive assistants knew you better than you knew yourself.

"Thanks," she said. "Please let him know I'm ready to see him."

Karl arrived ten minutes later. He looked tired, and she noticed he was wearing the same suit as the day before.

"Have you been up all night?"

He nodded. "Monitoring the protest from the command center," he said.

"Here, take this," she said, offering him the cappuccino.

"Thanks," he said, sipping gratefully.

She raised her eyebrows. "Why did the protest keep you from bed?"

He closed his eyes for a brief moment, appearing to center himself. Opening them again, he said, "Most of the time, keeping the peace is pretty mundane. It's about having a uniformed presence and striking the right balance in terms of enforcement so that people think twice before breaking the law. But sometimes, it gets out of hand. After a while, you start to see patterns. At first, you don't even notice. It just triggers a response in where and how you focus your attention. Eventually, you become more and more sensitive to those little details that just don't click."

He set down the empty cappuccino cup.

"Normally," he said, "protests run their course after a few hours. People get hungry, tired, cold, bored, whatever. They just sort of peter out. Sometimes they'll go on longer than that, but they usually break up late at night once people realize they're probably still going to have to go to work the next day. But last night, they didn't go home. They piled a bunch of old mattresses and worn-out tires at the intersection of Market and 40th Street and burned them."

As he was talking, Huian increased the opacity on the windows and brought up the feed, giving Karl control. He immediately cycled to a view from a drone hovering a few hundred meters above the demonstration.

Huian sucked in a breath. The dancing flames seemed to fill the entire intersection. Toxic black smoke roiled and billowed up from the blaze. Throngs of people were packed tight on the streets around it. More seemed to be filtering in even as they spoke.

"The bonfire is so big, it's melting the asphalt," said Karl. "They keep throwing more fuel on it."

He cycled through a variety of feeds. A man stood balanced on a sidewalk trash bin, giving some sort of rousing speech. Two dozen people were using spray paint and old cardboard boxes to make signs. A painfully cute toddler rode on his father's shoulders. Along the outer edges of the crowd, dreadlocked men stood with shotguns and assault rifles hanging from their shoulders.

"Who are *they*?" asked Huian, pointing. "Where are the police?"

"You can see the police there." He gestured off to the side, and she saw a group of police officers standing in front of their vehicles about a block away.

"They're certainly keeping their distance."

"They are," he said. "I've been on the line with the chief of police and Mayor Gonzalez twice this morning already. They are not eager to engage with the crowd given their resource constraints. Those armed men are members of Frederick O'Livier's organization. His group runs the Oakland Slums. Although they would never say as much, I get the distinct impression from the mayor that O'Livier may actually have more clout than he does. Their policy at the moment is live and let live. They're hoping it will eventually just die down."

"Wait, Frederick O'Livier? The guy who led the Warriors to the NBA Championships thirty years ago?" That had been one of the greatest postseasons ever played.

Karl nodded. "He transitioned from point guard to black-market mogul. To be fair to him, his men seem to be keeping things at least somewhat under control. They've been managing fuel additions to the fire so that it doesn't spread to the surrounding buildings. They stopped a few kids who were trying to loot a convenience story on Adeline and have broken up a few fights."

Looking closer, Huian saw that some of the armed men were actually wandering through the crowd handing out granola bars and bottled water. There was more going on here than met the eye. She needed to think, not just react. She needed to read between the lines.

"The crowd is much, much bigger than yesterday," she said.

"That's right," he said. "When night fell, we estimate there were five thousand protesters. As of this morning, there are approximately sixty-seven thousand people." He adjusted the feed to show a satellite view. She could see highlighted routes leading from all the Slums around the Bay Area that came together at the intersection. "The bonfire is the eye of the storm. At 7:15 this morning, we detected a dramatic uptick in the rate of influx of people. It went from a linear function to an exponential curve. My analysts expect that within the hour, there will be more than one hundred thousand people on the streets."

"Why? What triggered the change?"

Karl shifted on his feet, and Huian realized he was uncomfortable. "Ma'am, it seems to correlate with a provocative blog that posted at 7 a.m. Social channels are on fire with outraged chatter."

"Ma'am?" Tom's voice came over the intercom. "I have Chandra here. She's demanding to see you right away."

Chandra Patel was Cumulus's head of public relations. Huian shot a look at Karl and he shrugged.

"Send her in," she said.

The door opened immediately, and Chandra stalked into the office like a corporate lioness, black eyes ablaze against the smooth mahogany skin of her face. She didn't even bother to acknowledge Karl.

Chandra placed her hands on her hips. "We need to issue a statement," she said with enough voltage behind her words to kill. "And put this thing to rest before it gets *really* out of hand."

Huian raised her palms. "I'm still catching up," she said. "Bring me up to speed, and we'll figure out what to do."

Chandra looked at her incredulously for a moment and then composed herself.

"*This*," she said, bringing up an internet page on the display. It was plain text against a white background, no graphics, menu, or any kind of user interface. Just words.

Huian began to read.

29

"WHAT EXACTLY IS GOING ON HERE?" Frederick stood behind his reclaimed wood conference table, flanked by restless lieutenants.

Lilly stood opposite him with Henok and Penelope, the middle-aged woman in the denim jumpsuit from the day before, who turned out to be Frederick's computer science chief. The screens around the sides of the room displayed views from the protest, status reports from field commanders, and live satellite maps of the area.

Lilly briefed him on their experiments with the scanner and camera, laying the print photos of the man out on the table. Then she turned to Penelope.

"At first, we thought it must be user error or a simple bug," said the older woman. "That's what stuff like this almost always boils down to. But nobody on my team could figure out what was wrong. Then Danny pulled out an ancient iMac that isn't networked. We disconnected the scanners and hardwired them to the iMac. It worked perfectly. We could even print them as long as the printer was also disconnected from the network. Then we connected the iMac to the network and emailed the photos to ourselves. The emails failed to deliver. That's when we started getting suspicious. Just like everyone else, we connect to the internet via Bandwidth and all of our files are hosted on Backend. Bandwidth and Backend are both Cumulus companies. Our other computers and phones are all Cumulus as well, of course."

"Basically, whenever these photos touch the Cumulus ecosystem, they disappear," said Lilly, gesturing at the pictures on the table.

"And because the Cumulus ecosystem represents so much of the digital world, they are essentially invisible to all connected devices," said Henok.

Penelope nodded. "Danny also has that Cumulus admin exploit we've been hoarding. A friend of a friend scored it off a network administrator there in return for half a kilo of coke. I went ahead and used it. We tapped the Cumulus drone and satellite feeds, and Lilly showed us where and when to look. For example, we know the perp exited Sara's house through the back door and then exited to the street via the side yard. Then we have his path and approximate itinerary for the rest of the morning until he left Lilly. We can just scroll back to the right date and location, and start tracking him from there. Should be easy, right?"

Frederick rubbed his temples. "Your question implies it won't be."

"Check it out." Penelope turned and brought up a top-down image of Sara's house with a time stamp at the bottom showing it was the previous morning. A green Land Rover drove up the street and parked in the driveway.

"That's me," said Lilly.

On-screen, Lilly exited the truck and climbed the front steps, coffees in hand. A minute passed.

"Around now is when I saw him through the living room window and took this picture." Lilly indicated the photo on the table.

"But nobody's there," said Frederick, his frown deepening.

He was right. On screen, nothing changed until Lilly exited through the back door and dashed around the side of the house, slowing to a walk as she reached the sidewalk. She turned at the corner of the block.

"That's where I saw him again," she said and pointed to the next photo. Penelope fast-forwarded through time. On screen, Lilly made her way toward the West Oakland BART Station, apparently alone. Then she ducked behind a dumpster, occasionally peeking around it to snap a picture. "He was getting coffee from that street vendor," she said, holding up the next photo.

But on screen, the street vendor was alone. He just stood there stirring his pot and waiting for customers. Eventually, Lilly stepped out from behind the dumpster and hurried to the entrance of the West Oakland BART Station.

Penelope switched the feed to the North Berkeley Green Zone, and then played it forward through time. Lilly exited the BART station, passed the Security officers, and walked for a few blocks until she sat on a bench opposite the coffee shop. Lilly narrated for Frederick, and indicated the relevant photos she had taken along the way. Then she got up from the bench and walked a few more blocks before finding her hiding place behind the bougainvillea bushes. Other pedestrians made their way up the streets, but the man she was following was conspicuous only by his total absence.

I apologize if this is a little forward. But I think you've got a killer sense of style. According to the video surveillance, he had never entered or exited Dr. Corvel's office. He had never approached Lilly. No Fleet had ever pulled up beside her to whisk him away.

According to the video, the man didn't exist.

Frederick crossed his arms over his tuxedoed chest. The lines on his face had deepened. His lips were pressed together in a tight line.

There was a moment of silence.

Lilly took a shuddering breath. "If it weren't for these photos," she pressed both hands onto the tabletop, "I would be doubting my own sanity. But they're real. *He's* real."

The look Frederick gave her x-rayed her soul.

"I had my video guy take a look," said Henok. "It's subtle, but the footage has been doctored. Look at this." He rewound to the coffee vendor, zoomed in, and cycled backward and forward through time.

The vendor stirred the pot, tasted a sample, and looked around. Then he stirred the pot, tasted a sample, and looked around again. "It's a loop," said Henok, playing through it all again. "It's the same footage played back over itself and automatically meshed into all versions and angles from every Cumulus device. The video guy says that it's being done algorithmically. It's all automatic."

Penelope inserted a pencil into her mouth and started chewing on the end of it. "From what my compsci team can gather, the Cumulus system must have various tags identifying this guy—facial recognition, tracking his own devices, geolocation, anything associated with whatever stealth accounts he has. When the system sees a tag, it knows to wipe him from any data streams associated with that time and place, repairing the overall surveillance records with looped footage. That's why we don't see him on screen. Because he ordered the Fleet that pulled up next to Lilly, we don't see that Fleet on screen. It's been scraped completely—you can't even find it if you track back. That's also why Lilly wasn't able to photograph him from her Cumulus phone. And why we can't scan the photos. The minute they touch Cumulus, the system destroys them."

Frederick ran a finger along his chin. "So the only reason we have any evidence of his presence at all," he said, "is because—"

"Of this," said Lilly, holding up the camera slung around her neck. "This is a Yashica Lynx 14 with an aftermarket Russian ZENITAR lens. It's great for getting a nice shallow depth of field, perfect for black-and-white shots. But it's terrible for spyware that depends on every device being connected to the internet." She waggled the camera and couldn't suppress a grin. "The analog heel of a digital Achilles."

His lieutenants looked bemused but Frederick's forehead furrowed. "So, what we're really talking about here is a virtual phantom," he said. "A man invisible to the digital universe even as he's murdering people in the flesh. For a world dependent on digital investigative tools, he's essentially a ghost."

Lilly, Henok, and Penelope exchanged a glance. Frederick might not be technically inclined, but he had gotten the gist.

"In layman's terms," said Penelope, "that's not too far off the mark." She replaced the pencil in a pocket of her jumpsuit.

"Which begs the question," said Frederick, leaning across the table and impaling them with a fierce stare, "how do we find, expose, and destroy this motherfucker?"

Lilly raised a tentative hand.

"I have an idea," she said.

30

HUIAN RELEASED CHANDRA with orders to draft a statement, and Karl to monitor the situation from the command center.

Then she leaned against the edge of her desk and stared into the roaring flames that danced on the display. This was no good at all. These were the kinds of insurgencies that Cumulus would ultimately render irrelevant. This would never happen in the Green Zone. There would be no impetus for social uprising when society was fully optimized. Thankfully, even this bump in the road wouldn't affect the Green Zone communities. Karl had hundreds of armed Security officers stationed at every possible entrance. The chaos wouldn't spread beyond the Slums. And the Slums were chaotic to begin with.

Nevertheless, this was not something she wanted developing right in Cumulus's backyard. And she didn't know what to think about the connection to Sara Levine. A shadow fell over her soul. *Take care of them.* She had said that to Graham the evening Vera had left. The instruction was decidedly vague. But a certain level of ambiguity was necessary in sensitive situations. If anything had proved itself true over the years, it was that the only person she could truly rely on was herself. If the universe conspired to challenge her vision for

Cumulus, she needed to take commensurate action to defend that vision. It was simply too important to leave in the hands of fate.

The door behind her clicked shut softly. "I was just thinking of you," she said, turning.

Graham raised an eyebrow. He approached the desk, took a seat, and crossed one leg over the other. Huian was struck by the contrast with Chandra's entrance just an hour earlier. Where Chandra had charged into the room and immediately demanded Huian's attention, Graham's stride was measured and his demeanor calm and unassuming. His very lack of ardor was the most fascinating part of him.

She sat opposite him. "I assume you've been following the situation in West Oakland?"

He bobbed his head once.

"And?"

He raised that eyebrow again. "Demonstrations like this are not uncommon, particularly in areas with high Gini coefficients."

"Gini coefficients?"

"The most common ratio of economic inequality," he said. "A coefficient of zero means perfect income equality. Everyone makes precisely the same amount of money. A coefficient of one means perfect income inequality, one person captures all the income in a society and everyone else is left with nothing. The coefficient here in the States has been growing for decades. We've become more and more unequal. In terms of income inequality, we now more closely resemble Latin America than Western Europe. Whenever wealth is so unevenly distributed in a population, social tension is bound to arise. When social tension grows, protests and other forms of unrest simply become a part of the fabric of the nation."

Huian frowned. "I didn't request a lesson in economics. You know why I'm asking about the protest."

"What? Sara Levine?" Graham shook his head sadly. "A tragedy, isn't it? Cut off in the middle of a promising legal career. Very unfortunate. As to the protest, you never know what little spark might trigger this kind of thing. The straw that broke the camel's back, am I right?"

She drummed her fingers on the desktop. "Graham, when I told you to—"

"Ma'am?" he interrupted, uncrossing his legs and leaning forward. "If I may? I have helivaced VIPs out of war zones, overthrown dictators, and infiltrated foreign intelligence services. In short, I've been through a lot and worked with and against some of the most skilled and formidable professionals, alive and dead. In all that time, one golden rule has made itself ever more evident." He held up an index finger. "Policymakers must have plausible deniability. That means I will never confirm or deny information that might jeopardize you. Forgive the Beltway-speak, but you're the one making the calls and I'm the one solving the problems. Between us lies a sacred buffer, a line we should never cross. Just do your job and let me do mine."

Huian spun her chair 180 degrees and flicked the windows to fully transparent. Clouds were still scudding across the sky. High-altitude winds had taken their fluffy mass from earlier that morning and spread them out into long, paper-thin wisps. She could press him. But did she want to know the answers that lay below his imperturbable veneer? Even if she set aside potential criminal and civil liability, wouldn't that just be another form of micromanagement? From the day he'd walked into her office for the first time, she couldn't deny that Graham had always produced results. He had untangled that regulatory mess in Beijing, warned them of a potential executive hire's history of fraud, and given her timely insights into the operations of Cumulus's closest competitors. Plus, he always seemed to know things about her own direct reports even before she found out about them. Had it been wise to bring him on and approve the Ghost Program? Every leader needed someone they could really rely on. And he was right that geopolitical influence was migrating from its historic seat within national governments into the private sector. Beyond the windows, a flock of gulls glided over the Cumulus campus.

"Alright," she said, swiveling her chair back to face him. "I'll let you do your job. But be careful. We're a tech company, not a spy agency. I don't want us getting our hands dirty, and I certainly don't want blowback."

"Of course."

"And speaking of potential blowback, this protest is not good news. Whether or not you're right about economic inequality being the systemic problem, the fact is that Sara Levine's death sparked this whole thing. And that blog post tries to paint Cumulus into the picture."

He waved a hand. "It's all wildly circumstantial. The only thing that post does is say that she was working on a case targeting Cumulus and that she died. The only thing linking those two facts is a clever narrative."

"A clever narrative can go a surprisingly long way," she said. "Just ask any organized religion."

"It's bullshit and it's temporary," he said. "And it's anonymous. It's not even real journalism. Just wait for the next news cycle. Everyone will forget about it and move on."

"From what Chandra tells me, its anonymity is one of the reasons it's going viral. You may have a good rationale for not sharing the details of our involvement or lack thereof with any of this. But someone is trying to rope us into this mess, and we need to find out who they are. *You* need to find out who they are."

Graham touched two fingers to his forehead in a mock salute. "Your wish is my command."

"I think you're confusing Gini with genie."

31

LILLY GAZED OUT AT THE STREETS of her city as the truck rumbled along beneath her. The cab was a much higher vantage point than she was used to. It felt almost like she was looking down from a second-story window. The streets around the warehouse were empty. Everyone in the Slums was honing in on the protest, leaving their neighborhoods vacant. Trucks just like this one were going out to every part of every Slum in the Bay Area right now.

The preparations had taken all day. The amount of logistics required was impressive. Henok's design staff had been working nonstop to get every detail right on the different formats. They had monopolized every specialized printer they could get their hands on. Regional ink supplies were dwindling.

She was squeezed in beside the driver and Frederick. His organization used battered old trucks like this one because they were harder to track than Fleets, which were constantly connected. Frederick smelled faintly of rosemary. It was his people who had orchestrated the production, and his money that had paid for it. As soon as the prints had dried, groups of men piled them into trucks on the loading dock of the warehouse. One truck would rumble off, and an empty one would take its place, its cavernous bed ready for more pieces of what was perhaps the most ambitious public art project ever attempted.

Lilly turned her head to the passenger window to hide a grin. She had always felt apart. Having dead parents will do that to a person. She had been only twenty when they died. As soon as the press found out that the other vehicle had been a self-driving car, they had turned what should have been a family tragedy into a media circus. Lilly's friends and relatives hadn't known what to do with her. Every conversation had been tainted by undercurrents of pity and awkwardness. Lilly couldn't blame them. And, to their credit, she had always been a bit of a loner. Not in the sense that she didn't enjoy the company of others. She just never understood why she should do what society seemed to expect from her. She had no interest in engineering, business, law, medicine, or any of the other subjects that offered real career paths. She had fallen in love with photography on that day in high school. That passion hadn't waned. But what were you supposed to do as an unemployed twenty-year-old who loved taking pictures with retro equipment?

She used Lancer to land whatever jobs she could. Weddings ended up being the only thing that helped her make ends meet. But shooting weddings deepened her isolation. Anybody who worked service jobs could attest to the same thing. All these people were as happy as they could be and surrounded by loved ones. Most partied hard. They paid Lilly to capture the joy she didn't share. They weren't her friends. They were a happy group of wealthy strangers who forced her to think how inadequate her meager existence really was. They were popping bottles of expensive champagne while she was looking forward to a lonely dinner of instant noodles in a cramped apartment deep in the Slums. She knew much of it was her own fault. If she had wanted to make money, she should have studied up to become an attorney, engineer, or financier. But no matter how centered she tried to be, it was difficult to prevent resentment from slinking into her subconscious.

Sara's death was still too shocking to process. Lilly couldn't believe she would never see her friend again. But she felt a strange sense of fierce pride. When she saw what had happened to Sara, Lilly hadn't just frozen in panic or collapsed into a blubbering mess. She had taken action. She had shadowed the killer. She had gone to the police. She had gone *beyond* the police. Now, she was making a real difference and increasing the pressure for the investigation to yield real results. She had uncovered key evidence, and was helping put together the puzzle that seemed to lurk behind this entire debacle. And with these pictures, she would go from a fly on the wall to a fly in the ointment. That was something Sara would respect. You didn't throw yourself at the mercy of justice. Justice helped those who helped themselves.

"What are you thinking about?" Frederick nudged her with his shoulder.

Lilly looked up at the lined russet-brown face above the tuxedo. He really *was* tall. Seated next to him, her head barely reached his shoulder.

"I was just wondering what Sara might think of all this," she said.

Pain flashed behind Frederick's eyes. "The thought had occurred to me too." He put his hand over hers and gave it a squeeze. "Sara never liked it when I tried to speak for her. She hated other people putting words in her mouth. But I can only imagine that if she had seen a friend killed, she would stop at nothing to get to the bottom of it. I've never met a person more tenacious than she was. My dogs could have taken a few pointers from her in that department."

Lilly stared at him for a long moment. "What do you want?" she asked.

The corners of his lips turned down. "More than anything," he said, soulful exhaustion behind the words, "I'd like to retire."

A half dozen police cruisers were parked haphazardly across the street in front of them. Their lights were flashing but their sirens were silent. The old truck pulled up, and an officer stepped forward. The driver rolled down the window, but Frederick leaned over before he could speak. The police officer's eyes widened when he saw Frederick in the cab, and he waved them through without a word.

The truck had to roll one wheel up onto a curb in order to get around the police cars, whose flashing lights had blinded them to the scene beyond. It took a moment for Lilly's eyes to adjust as they thumped back onto the street on the other side. The truck pulled forward another few hundred meters and then stopped. The driver left the engine running.

They disembarked from the cab, and Lilly got her first clear look at what was going on. The street ahead of them was an ocean of tightly packed people. It went on for blocks and blocks and blocks. Toddlers, teenagers, and grandmothers of every shape and color. Far off in the distance, the central bonfire blazed above the heads of the assembled multitudes. It was late afternoon, and the sun was just starting to dip below the horizon. Dusk threw shadows everywhere, and turned the vast cloud of smoke issuing from the fire into a tower of deep purple that stretched impossibly high above them. A constant, unending buzz made the crowd seem like a living organism. It was like the audience chattering in anticipation before a sold-out stadium show.

Five of Frederick's dreadlocked enforcers stood at the edge of the crowd facing out toward the waiting police. Lilly imagined similar scenes must be playing themselves out on the hundreds of other streets that led into the multiple square kilometers of city the protest now occupied. They recognized Frederick, and one hurried over to greet them, shotgun dangling from its shoulder strap.

"Sir," he said. "It's starting to get out of control in the northeast. We don't have enough men stationed there to keep the crowd back."

Frederick's expression turned grim. "We knew that would happen eventually. How far have they gotten?"

"They just hit the Fringe."

"Well, at least it's not our territory," said Frederick. "Remember your orders. Our duty here is to protect the people. Property damage is deplorable, but we will not tolerate violence directed at our citizens."

The man bumped a fist on his chest. "Yes, sir."

"Now," said Frederick. "Can you give us a hand unloading this truck?"

32

THE MILK SLOUGHED OFF crystals of sugar and cinnamon as it flowed down over the mountain of CTC piled high in the bowl. It formed swirling eddies as it pooled and eroded the pyramid of cereal. Little by little, the mass disintegrated until the entire thing finally collapsed into the churning milk.

You know why I'm asking about the protest. Graham had to admit that his last conversation with Huian had put him on edge. The demonstration itself wasn't a problem. It was an inevitable side effect of their era. Let the disenfranchised burn off some steam and break a few windows. But the timing had been bad luck and the blog post worse. He had expected Sara's assassination to be written off as yet another Slum homicide. Killings were so frequent and unremarkable in the Slums that he hadn't suspected this one would attract undue attention. The stack of OPD cold cases was sky-high. But Sara had been some kind of folk hero, and her neighbors had taken to the streets. Even that wouldn't have lasted as long as it had without direct support from local gang affiliates. Now their efforts were making the futile search for Sara's killer into a cause célèbre.

If Sara had lived in the Green Zone, he would have expected her death to create a scandal. There hadn't been a Green Zone homicide for three years running, and Security had a nearly perfect conviction rate before that. When every device was an extension of Cumulus's eyes and ears, investigations were pretty straightforward. Security could just access Cumulus data on the victim's phone or any connected devices, vehicles, or drones in the area. Just scroll back through time, and you could see exactly who the perpetrator was, and proceed from there to follow every digital breadcrumb they had ever left.

Security didn't have jurisdiction in the Slums, and OPD didn't have access to Cumulus data. But even if OPD detectives were able to win access by using the publicity angle to convince a judge to force the issue, Graham was still untouchable. That's why the blog post and the protest made him nervous but didn't send him into a panic. This was precisely the kind of contingency he had designed the Ghost Program to defend against.

Law enforcement and intelligence organizations depended on digital tools to aid their physical surveillance and investigative efforts. Every agency on earth had grown complacent with such easy data at their fingertips. Their human intelligence capacities withered on the vine. But with the Ghost Program in place, those tools would be useless against Graham. His special status as a digital wraith made him virtually invisible. They could dig through every archive but wouldn't find him anywhere. Every trace of his presence was automatically wiped clean by specially designed algorithms.

Graham rubbed his eyes. He had been staring at a screen for too long. The gray light of pre-dawn was just starting to filter through the windows of his apartment. He filled a fresh mug of coffee, picked up the bowl of cereal, and returned to his desk.

Infiltrating Cumulus had been many times easier than winning access to many of the cadres that he had been charged with cracking over the years. In fact, counterintelligence measures were so weak that Graham himself had gotten lazy about them. He didn't even bother with SDRs anymore. Surveillance detection runs were standard practice prior to running an op. The agent would combine pedestrian, private, and public transit in a way designed to flush out any followers. You'd take the subway, get off the train, and wait in the station until everyone else had moved on and then take the train back in the other direction, forcing anybody shadowing you to come out in the open. You'd take elevators to various floors and then leave through different exits. You'd walk up one-way streets against traffic to throw off anyone following you in a vehicle. After moving to San Francisco, Graham had run SDRs here for the first few months out of force of habit, but it quickly became clear that they were nothing but a waste of time. With the Ghost Program in place, who cared? Why bother with an SDR when you were already invisible to a potential enemy's drone? He carried the ultimate get-out-of-jail-free card.

But with the events of the last forty-eight hours, Graham knew he needed to be more careful. He had become too reliant on his ace-in-the-hole, using it as a crutch instead of a superpower. Granddad would have been disgusted with his negligence. From now on, he would increase his security precautions. The Ghost Program had saved him from an otherwise disastrous scandal. There was no need to press his luck. Inconvenient as they were, he'd run SDRs on all ops from now on. His enemies might be civilians, but even amateurs got lucky every once in a while. No need to make it easy for them.

He sat down at the desk. His display showed live coverage of the protest. This would be the third straight day. Last night, the crowd had invaded the Fringe, and turned into a riot. They were looting the hipster coffee shops, coworking spaces, luxury condos, cocktail bars, and gourmet restaurants that clung to the edge of the Green Zone like barnacles. They had somehow surrounded a number of Fleets and had set the vehicles on fire. The main thrust of the crowd was surging up 40th Street toward MacArthur BART Station. MacArthur BART was a raised station built in the center of Highway 24, which ran perpendicular to 40th Street and constituted the border between the Fringe and the Green Zone in that part of North Oakland.

Security had fortified the overpass at the intersection of Highway 24 and 40th Street. They had spray-painted a green line across the asphalt, demarcating their jurisdiction. Hundreds of Security officers in full riot gear stood at attention under the overpass, the boots of the vanguard just centimeters behind the line. The first wave of protesters was only about thirty meters from that line, holding back but jeering at the waiting officers. Security had shut down Highway 24 entirely, and sharpshooters brandished high-powered assault rifles atop it, using the highway guardrails as ramparts. Drones supported them from the sky, and Security vehicles were lined up in orderly rows on the Green Zone side of the highway. Security had also called for a voluntary curfew within the Green Zone, and had already evacuated people living close to the border.

Graham shook his head and took a bite of CTC, washing it down with a mouthful of coffee. He had been in enough burgeoning riots to know that this would not end well. When tension got this high, all you needed was one idiot to make a mistake, and things would go to hell in a handbasket. Huian had received separate calls from the governor and the president. The former was trying to mobilize the National Guard, but that would take far too long. The president was terrified of seeing a catastrophe developing when the country was only one year away from a national election. Karl was on the line with Mayor Gonzalez and the OPD chief for hourly updates. But their efforts would be too little, too late.

He stood behind what he had told Huian. The real issue here was the country's long descent into inequality. The changes he had noticed whenever he returned to his homeland had quietly fermented, a vat of perceived social injustice. If you wanted to avert this kind of situation, you needed to start *way* earlier by correcting the socioeconomic shift. They hadn't. Which was totally expected. Why would powerful incumbents want to rock the boat and upset a pecking order that benefitted them? The only difference here was that American leaders had gotten soft. They had won their positions in a country that didn't yet require an iron hand. The middle class had fallen victim to the death of a thousand cuts. With them had died the nation's solidarity. Now, those leaders felt uncomfortable because they had put themselves in an untenable situation. They lacked the nerve to do what needed doing. Violence was rearing its ugly head, and they were tying themselves up in knots over it. Leaders more accustomed to ruling societies with these kinds of demographics would never have been caught with their pants down. They would have put this to rest on day one with a few well-timed displays of shock-and-awe force. Nothing made joining a protest less appealing than intermittent raids by ruthless strike teams.

Graham ate another spoonful of CTC, slurping the milk so it didn't drip down his chin. Violence didn't make him uncomfortable. This was exactly what he had been expecting. It was blindingly obvious. But it was called *blindingly* obvious for a reason. These kinds of situations were his professional forte. Moments of chaos were tipping points. History books imagined that change happened in smooth arcs, but Graham knew better. Ninety-nine percent of history was essentially static. Incumbent players competed for incremental gains. But the other one percent—that's where things got interesting. Circumstances would shift so radically that century-long assumptions would be turned over in a day. Most people were so caught up in those assumptions that they wouldn't even realize it was happening. But the few who did could leapfrog from street urchin to robber baron. Or from lowly intelligence agent to the corporate overlord.

He lifted the bowl to drink the last of the sugary milk left in the bottom. His long-laid plans were finally bearing fruit. Huian was ensnared in concentric circles of traps. He was engineering her world from the inside out in a psychological architecture that gave him total control. She had been easy to subvert. Success in Silicon Valley was unusual by geopolitical standards because it did not entirely depend on the classic mix of refined paranoia and megalomania. Huian was fundamentally a builder, not a ruler. And that distinction left her vulnerable to people with Graham's skills and mindset.

He smiled and finished the last sip of coffee. When this little piece of action was over, he really deserved to get himself laid. Sex might be nothing more than a temporary reprieve from the vagaries of life in the shadows, but that didn't mean he needed to give himself blue balls. Maybe he'd track down that Japanese-looking piece of ass he'd seen after leaving Dr. Corvel's office. She was seriously hot and so shy that she had demurred to respond when he had approached and complimented her. Visions of alabaster skin and entangled limbs rose in his mind. He shook himself. Yes, he'd track her down once this was over. That would be easy. Hell, he could trawl through her account history and find footage of her in the shower if he wanted to. But pussy could wait. Right now, he had work to do.

He clicked away from the protest feeds and back to his latest research project. Huian had tasked him with finding out who was behind that anonymous blog post, and he had spent the last day and night working back through a series of digital clues to identify the undisclosed author.

The hunt had proved surprisingly challenging. Whoever posted the essay knew their cybersecurity. They had used TOR and dozens of straw man accounts to obscure all of the originating IP addresses and servers involved. That might have put them out of reach if Graham were operating on his own. But he had all of Cumulus at his fingertips, and his root access gave him insights into the plumbing of the internet that not even the NSA could match. Coffee and CTC had fueled his obsessive pursuit until he had identified that the article had been posted from a warehouse in West Oakland known as the Compound.

The Compound was the headquarters of Frederick O'Livier, the NBA-star-turned-mafioso who had so adeptly turned the murder of his girlfriend into a political hot potato. Graham remembered standing in Huian's office, describing Sara Levine and the threat her lawsuit posed to Cumulus. *Jesus, Graham. Is she fucking right now? Is this how you get off?* When he had pulled up the live feed from her phone, the grunts and moans of intercourse had piped over Huian's speakers. He snorted. Frederick must have been on top of her, pumping away. A day later, Graham had put two bullets into her right in the middle of the bitch's living room.

The best part was that Sara had let him in the door herself. He had been feeding her the information she needed to make a case against Cumulus, and so when he proposed meeting at her place to reveal his identity, she had enthusiastically accepted. Civilians could be so stupid. She was used to dealing with whistleblowers and disgruntled employees, not professionals. She was trying to set up Cumulus without realizing that she was the one being set up.

Now, her capo boyfriend was abetting the Slummer protest to leverage some kind of advantage out of her killing. Revenge for his fuck-buddy was one thing. But even better if it gave him another piece of ammunition in the ongoing skirmishes with other gangs and politicians that he must be constantly involved in. Plus, it was the perfect opportunity to unify his base of Slummers in outrage over an injustice suffered by an upstanding member of the community. No wonder he sponsored the blog post. It was ideal propaganda that played right into the resentment that all Slummers felt at a system that seemed to lock them out at every turn.

Let Frederick make his gambit. Graham didn't mind. This kind of anarchy afforded Graham more leeway for making aggressive moves, stratagems that would otherwise be too risky. When everyone's eyes were glued to news feeds, they weren't watching their own backs. But that would be for later. Right now, the demonstrations had already offered him something extremely valuable. He now had the opportunity to solidify Huian's trust. When things looked like they were getting out of control, she had turned to him for counsel and support. This was the perfect time to demonstrate the efficacy of his methods by delivering exactly what she wanted. She would have yet another proof point that when he made a promise, he delivered. He was her lifeline now that she was becoming ever more personally and professionally isolated. The alienated crave human connection more than anything else. Graham would be her connection, and she would become his puppet. And if the carrot didn't work, he had been sharpening a special stick just for her.

A notification pinged, and Graham clicked over to another tab. Perfect. The semantic pattern recognition check was complete. He had taken the text of the blog post and run it through a set of algorithms built to identify the unique combination of markers that every writer left in their compositions. Grammatical oddities. Turns of phrase. Word choice. Variance in sentence and paragraph length. Unusual usage. Stylistic bent. Punctuation habits. Given a large enough sample, writing was as identifiable as a fingerprint. Noms de plume be damned.

A list of articles populated his screen. He clicked through and scanned them in order. My, oh my, the previously anonymous author was a prolific fellow. He had penned features in major magazines, investigative reports for think tanks, personal essays taking a populist stance on various political issues, and hundreds of blog posts. Henok Addisu was a busy man. Three years ago, he had even written a long-form profile on Frederick O'Livier for the *New York Times Magazine.* The story focused more on O'Livier's efforts at community engagement than on his criminal enterprise. Might Frederick, sensing a kindred spirit, have asked him to assist with this delicate and provocative exposé?

Graham pulled up all the background he could find on Henok. Data flashed across his screen. Photos that ran from when he was a child all the way up to the present. Résumé, job, and educational history. Medical and financial information. Living and dead family members. Closest friends and affiliates ranked by proximity and depth of social media engagement. Graham didn't try to read everything. He skimmed as quickly as he could, and tried to let a picture of Henok form in his mind. First-generation American born to Ethiopian immigrant parents. A skilled reporter who was frustrated with the lack of vision of his newsroom editorial bosses. Graham could identify with that. Henok tried working for a few lower-tier outlets only to discover that while they were willing to offer creative freedom, they didn't have the resources to let him pursue real stories. Eventually, he hung up his spurs and jumped over to the public relations dark side to help Frederick O'Livier, a previous interviewee, manage his reputation. Once in a while, he was able to pick up the pen to draft articles that furthered the interests of his employer.

Henok had no idea how much trouble he was in. He probably thought it was ever so clever how they had purged the article of anything that might identify him. Graham shook his head. The kid had a long way to go before he became a hard target. It was almost cute. Almost.

Time to take a peek into Henok's world.

Graham tunneled through Cumulus to locate Henok's phone. A satellite map zoomed in. North America. West Coast. California. Bay Area. Oakland. The Compound. No surprises there. Cameras from drones in nearby airspace gave Graham multiple angles on the building. Murals covered the walls. Armed guards stood at every gate. A pack of dogs roamed the asphalt no-man's-land between the building and the barbed-wire fences surrounding it. This guy got to work early—it was just before 7 a.m.

Graham played the live feed from the phone itself. Two windows popped up on his screen, views from the front and back cameras. Both were completely black. It took Graham a moment to digest. It was either in a pocket, or the cameras were blocked somehow. The GPS indicated that the phone was right in the middle of the warehouse. The audio cut in but sounded muffled, nothing but indistinct voices. Cranking up the volume didn't help. He triangulated for other phones in the vicinity. All muffled. Damn. They must be using security precautions. Layering audio feeds from the nearby phones on top of each other, he eliminated all sounds that didn't fall into the human vocal spectrum to increase the signal-to-noise ratio. Knitting the clean files together, he cranked up the volume again. Gotcha.

"—ready for this?" Automatically transcribed words flowed up Graham's screen as he heard a man's voice.

"As ready as we'll ever be," said a female voice. "Frederick's deployment teams have nearly all reported in. It took us all night to distribute and put up, but we've got as much coverage as we're going to get in every format we could dream up." Her tone had a hint of wonder. "It still blows my mind that this kind of thing is even possible."

The man chuckled in a way that confirmed the sense of awe. "When Frederick sets his mind to something, he goes all in. I guess you don't become an NBA champion by relying on half measures." The voice-recognition software confirmed that this was Henok speaking. Got him. "Given how much of a splash yesterday's post made, I can't even imagine what's going to happen once this gets out. I've got to say, when you told me about the pictures yesterday, I had no idea they were going to constitute a story as big as their subject. I officially retract any fun I poked at your retro equipment. I guess that classics are classic for a reason."

Graham's pulse accelerated. What were they talking about? A new post? What could that mean? Were they going to release a follow-up to yesterday's incendiary story? If so, what would it be about? He forced himself to take a deep breath. No matter how clever these kids thought they were, he was safe. They could write all the social justice rants they wanted to, but they would never be able to directly implicate him.

"Real women change their own oil." Pride shone through her words.

"Then I'd make a terrible woman," said Henok. Graham silently willed him to shut up. The software needed more samples from the woman before it could find a voice-recognition match. "Oh, and I'm going to demand a signed copy of one of those photos. I have a feeling I might be the first to ask for your autograph, but I won't be the last."

Graham's brow furrowed. What photos? Pictures of Sara's corpse, maybe? Why would that matter? Again, he forced himself to calm down. No photos of him were anywhere on the internet, nor could they be. He was probably the only human alive with essentially no online presence. Of course, he maintained various false identities that he could activate when needed. Those profiles had digital debris that verified their existences. But they were nothing but fluff. The Ghost Program was a damn-good security blanket. The NSA probably wouldn't even be able to get past it.

"Only if you hand-write me a copy of your story."

"With papyrus and quill, milady." Their banter was painful.

"Will you hit publish already?" Voice recognition got a hit: Lilly Miyamoto.

Graham heard a tap.

"Done," said Henok.

Curiosity piqued, Graham pulled up the URL of the first anonymous blog post. Sure enough, there was now a Part Two. He muted the audio surveillance feed so that he could read it without distraction. There might be some tidbits in here that he could use to his advantage. Because he had heard them publish it live, he would be one of the very first people to see the post. Maybe he'd contact Huian immediately afterwards to tell her about it. That would further the impression of omniscience he was making. Yes, that was a good idea. He'd report in after finishing it.

Graham began to read and the world disintegrated around him.

The article told the story of a friend of Sara's who visited her the morning of the murder. The friend walked in the front door to discover the corpse and then saw a stranger leaving through the property's side gate. It went on to relate Graham's entire morning. The friend had shadowed him all the way to Corvel's and related everything in excruciating detail. They claimed to have taken many pictures along the way. Unable to scan the photos, they had tried every means at their disposal to get them loaded online. Thanks to the Ghost Program, every attempt had been unsuccessful. Then they had broken into Cumulus remotely and accessed device data records to discover that Graham had been erased from all footage. Screen-captured video clips highlighted the inconsistencies left by the automatic Ghost Program edits. They had even deployed an open-source piece of pattern-recognition software called Mozaik to identify the variables targeted by Ghost Program algorithms. All of the code and raw results were shown as sidebars to the body of the article. Then the story referenced the previous day's post to highlight how Sara had been investigating Cumulus and how much the company stood to gain from her death. It deduced that either Cumulus was complicit in the assassination and hiding the perpetrator, or that a professional killer had found a way to circumvent the system that society relied upon for security.

The story concluded by telling readers they could see it for themselves by using their phones to try to upload digital pictures of the thousands of prints that had been installed overnight on billboards, telephone poles, signs, flyers, and buildings around the Bay Area. It asked them to report and apprehend the man in the pictures. It asked anyone with the right expertise to continue their research into how this was possible and publicize the results. They would take down a digital conspiracy with analog weapons. They would find the murderer and ensure that Sara's legacy of fighting for the dispossessed would live on.

Sick fascination forced Graham to read through to the very last word. He was paralyzed in the same way as when he'd watched the boy burn in the depths of the Malaysian rainforest, the binoculars melting into the charred husk of his adolescent corpse. He felt like the protagonist of a Kafka novel, unable to tear himself away from a nightmare spinning further and further out of control. Bile rose in his throat. His hands were shaking so hard that he knocked the cereal bowl and coffee mug off the desk. They shattered on impact, sending ceramic shards ricocheting across the floor.

If his cover was blown, he was completely fucked. This wasn't some throw-away fake identity that he could ditch while he hopped on the next flight out of the country. He had played all his cards and seized the reins of power at Cumulus. You couldn't just walk away once you'd won. That was unthinkable.

No, no, no. This couldn't be real. His deepest fears were creeping out from his subconscious to perform a nightmarish shadow play. It was some sort of bad dream. Enough. Time to wrest himself from the clutches of sleep. He snatched a jagged piece of cereal bowl off the floor and dug the ragged edge into his opposite forearm. Pain exploded in a blinding white flash. But when his vision cleared, he was still sitting at his desk. He tried again, harder this time. Nerves screamed in protest, and blood pumped from the open gashes. But the blog post still glowed on the screen in front of him.

A tiny spark of hope flashed in his mind. Even if he was forced to scrap the Ghost Program, he still had enough leverage over Huian to continue to bend her to his will. It would be ugly but it could work. The blog post showed only his absence, not Graham himself. If he could keep his true identity, his face, from coming out, then he still had a chance. Obscurity was his most valuable asset. He could jettison the rest, and his plans might still survive.

But the post had also mentioned pictures. Pictures that had already been distributed across the Bay Area. What did those pictures actually show? He needed to find out.

Graham gripped the edge of the desk and pushed himself to his feet. Blood poured down his arm and dripped off his fingers. He stumbled out into the living room. Wrenching the French doors open, he lurched onto the balcony. The article had said they were *everywhere*. He scanned the view with maniacal intensity. For a second, nothing appeared to be out of place and he almost sighed with relief.

Then a far off movement caught his eye. Something dropped from the lower deck of the Bay Bridge. It was a rolled up piece of textile, its top corners secured to the metal trusses. The fabric unfurled into the size and shape of a football field as it fell from the deck. The wind whipped at the bottom corners, but they were weighted to keep it from flapping around like a flag. It took a moment for Graham to resolve the image printed on the fabric. Then he dropped to his knees. He grasped the bars of the railing, slippery in his bloody grip. The universe spun around him like a horrific kaleidoscope.

His own face stared back at him. The photographer had captured him just as he was glancing over his shoulder to check out the ass of that passing jogger. Tearing his gaze away from the bridge, Graham sought out the various billboards around downtown San

Francisco that he could see from his balcony. Normally, they displayed ads promising Green Zone real estate, Fleet convenience, and Lancer opportunities. But they had all changed overnight. Sara's gruesome corpse lay on her couch. Graham hustled away from her house. The street vendor served him coffee. He stood on the West Oakland BART platform waiting for the next train. He entered the café in Berkeley and exited wearing different clothes. He stepped out through the door of Corvel's office.

This couldn't be happening. He had abandoned his career at the Agency to seek his fortune at Cumulus. It had taken years of preparation and diligent execution. He was just now beginning to reap the fruits of that labor. These pictures jeopardized everything. *Everything.* His face was plastered around the entire city. His crime was exposed. His cover was blown. His dreams turned to ash from one second to the next. This couldn't be happening.

Someone was responsible for this. Someone took those pictures. Someone followed him and accidentally circumvented the Ghost Program by using a fucking antique camera. They were excising the heart of the most sophisticated intelligence operation in history with a relic from the twentieth century. The blog post had described a friend of Sara's who discovered her body. *I'm going to demand a signed copy of one of those photos. I have a feeling I might be the first to ask for your autograph, but I won't be the last.* Henok had said that. He had been talking to whoever did this. They had published the article together.

Graham squeezed the slick bars and scrambled to his feet. Lilly Miyamoto. The voice-recognition program had identified her. He tripped as he dashed back through the living room and fell hard, grunting in pain as he landed on his injured arm. Motherfucker. He stood again and stalked the last few meters to his office.

Lilly Miyamoto. Time to see exactly who the fuck she thought she was. He brought up her full Cumulus profile and froze as her face materialized on his screen. He knew her. He fucking knew this bitch. *I apologize if this is a little forward. But I think you've got a killer sense of style.* The hot girl with Japanese features he had seen under the bougainvillea bushes after leaving Corvel's office. He had boarded a Fleet when it pulled up at the curb behind her, riding away and imagining how it might feel to get his hands under her clothes. Holy shit. That's where she had been photographing him from. She had been following him all morning, shooting the pictures that predicated his downfall.

He scanned through her profile, searching for clues that might tell him who had hired her. It had to be the Agency. Fuck, no. Maybe the Chinese had found out how he'd pulled the wool over their eyes. It could be Mossad or even BIN seeking some kind of vengeance for the Pulau Wei hit. But her profile was clean. Parents killed in a car crash, both Japanese expat engineers living in San Diego. Lilly had moved to Oakland to seek her fortune as a photographer and eked out a living shooting vintage photos of Greenie weddings. She lived in a studio apartment in the West Oakland Slums. Friends with Sara Levine, took care of her truck for her. Grocery and restaurant receipts showed a ramen obsession. No arrests. No known affiliations with foreign governments or private security firms. So perhaps she was working for some new player that Graham hadn't yet encountered. Someone who understood enough about cybersecurity to fabricate this clean Lilly identity for his agent to use. Someone like Graham. They must have realized how he had conquered Cumulus, and wanted to move against him while they still could.

He pulled the geolocation on Lilly's phone. With one roll of film, she had wrecked his ambitions beyond repair. Revenge was poor compensation. But he would take what he could get.

33

"MA'AM?"

Huian rolled over and tried to rub the sleep from her eyes.

"Ma'am?" The voice came through the speakers.

"Tom? What time is it?"

"Ma'am, I'm so sorry to wake you," said Tom. "It's 6 a.m."

Alright, so she had slept for two and a half hours. She swung her legs over the side of the bed, and rolled her head around to work out the kinks in her neck.

"Ma'am, I wouldn't have disturbed you but Martín Sanchez is here to see you."

"You mean here in person?"

"He's standing right here in front of me."

What on earth was Martín Sanchez doing here at six in the morning? They had never even met in person before. What could he possibly want that couldn't wait until a normal hour? Well, at least this would be a welcome respite from the thorny issue of managing the protest. She could do with something simple like a business negotiation. Maybe Martín's board had pressured him into accepting her acquisition offer. If so, that was a coup for Cumulus. It established yet another cog in her architecture of the future. It would give them access to an entirely new class of data, and make Cumulus integral to the operations of the energy industry. She could leverage that to get the concessions and operating licenses they'd been fighting for in the Gulf for so long.

"Give me five minutes," she said.

"Yes, ma'am."

Huian washed her face, brushed her teeth, and pulled on a fresh set of clothes. Yes. Whatever it was Martín was here for, it was better than overthinking a politically fraught demonstration. She mentally reviewed the terms, economics, and other details of the Tectonix acquisition. She would probably be able to reduce the offer price now that Martín was presumably coming to the table with a mandate from his directors. If they were already committed to selling the company and had forced Martín's hand, then she didn't need to double their original offer price to get the better of his pride. He had already turned that deal down and forfeited the terms. A fresh page was a fresh page.

She stepped out into her office. The gray fingers of dawn were just starting to creep past the eastern horizon. She picked up the worn basketball from the desk and spun it on a fingertip, making constant adjustments to keep it balanced and in motion. Executing against a long-term vision was a delicate thing. It required the right mix of patience and audacity. She worked hard to get the best information possible, but had to make major decisions in the face of paralyzing uncertainty. Try as she might, it wasn't something she could delegate.

"Send him in," she said.

The door opened, and Martín Sanchez stepped through. He had on a sharp formal suit and burgundy tie. She returned the basketball to the desk and stepped forward to greet him. Up close, he looked like shit. Bags sagged under his eyes. Lines creased his face. His palm was sweaty when they shook hands. A muscle in his cheek twitched. The board must have really put him through the ringer this time.

"I will give you what you want," he said. "I have board approval to negotiate the acquisition."

"That's wonderful," said Huian. This was going to be easier than she had anticipated. She would need to remember not to have Martín manage any buy-side deals once he was one of her operating executives. By playing his cards this quickly, he was ceding his negotiating position. Regardless, this was incredible news. After a few days of nothing but putting out fires, it was a blessing to have something going right. "I meant it when I invited you to become a part of the Cumulus family. I think you'll find a good home for Tectonix here. We'd be thrilled to have your team on board, and of course, I would depend on you to continue to lead and inspire them. Come, sit." She waved him to a chair. "Let's work out the logistics and get the ball rolling."

An ugly look flashed across his face, and he raised both hands. "No, I'm good standing," he said. "And you can dispense with the fluffy horseshit. I could have had my lawyers relay this information and define the terms. But I came here in person to let you know that I used to respect you. We never met, but I watched you lead Cumulus's meteoric rise. It was inspiring. It was one of the reasons I decided to start Tectonix in the first place."

His expression turned into a snarl. "But now I know the truth," he said. "You're not a builder, you're a bully. Cumulus isn't a company, it's a cartel. A syndicate you hold together through intimidation and blackmail. You want to tear apart my company and my family at the same time? Okay, you win. I'm not the kind of person who's willing to throw his own daughter to the dogs. So take my company, ravage my life's work. But don't you dare pretend you're playing nice while you're doing it. And don't send errand boys to manipulate me. That's the lowest kind of deceit. If you're going to fuck me over, do it in person."

His entire body trembled as he took in a ragged breath. The basketball rolled off the desk and dribbled to a stop in the corner.

Huian's expression was slack. For a moment, she couldn't do more than just stare at him. Then she found her voice.

"What on earth are you talking about?" she said.

Martín's eyes narrowed. He spat and Huian looked down in disbelief to see the glob of saliva dripping off her shoe.

He squared his shoulders, turned, and exited the way he had come.

Huian stared after him, too stunned to react.

"Ma'am?" Tom poked his head around the door jamb, concerned.

"Get Graham on the line," she said, trying to pull herself together. As head of her intelligence service, he better know what the fuck this was about. "Now."

"But, ma'am—"

"Out of my way, boy." Karl shouldered past Tom and into her office. His face looked as if it had been carved from solid granite. He looked at Huian.

"The shooting's started," he said.

34

LILLY SUPPRESSED A YAWN. She had spent the entire night out with Frederick in the truck, delivering printed signs, billboard supplies, and flyers. The stranger's face was now everywhere around the Bay Area. It was plastered on empty walls, posted on telephone poles, illustrated on T-shirts, and hanging from the Bay Bridge on a massive banner. The URL for Henok's story was highlighted on each print. Despite the gravity of the situation, she couldn't help but feel exhilarated. She was contributing to something important. Her art mattered. It was how she could help seek justice for Sara. But now that she was sitting beside Henok at his desk in the warehouse, she could barely keep her eyes open. "Ma'am?" The voice came through the speakers.

Henok glanced over at her. "You need to get some sleep," he said.

"No," she said. "There's too much—" She yawned against her will. "There's too much to do."

"It's settled," said Henok. "You're going home to rest for a few hours. There is literally nothing either of us can do right now. We just published the post, and it will take another day before the printers catch up with the demand for more photos, assuming we even need more."

He grabbed her hands and pulled her to her feet. "Come on," he said. "I'll order you a Fleet. You can get some shut-eye and then come back around midday."

"But—"

"Seriously," he said, rounding on her with a fierce look. "You need a nap." Then his expression softened. "Oh, I'm sorry. You probably don't want to be alone at your apartment at a time like this. With what happened to Sara and all. I'll go talk to Frederick and find you a place to lie down."

"No, it's not that," she said. The emotional aftermath of her friend's death was tinged with more anger than fear. It was easier to fill the void of Sara's absence with action than grief. "There's just so much happening right now. So many things I can help with."

Henok's expression turned stern again. "I promise I will call you if anything important happens, okay?"

She wanted to argue with him, but she knew he was right. She didn't have the energy for a debate anyway.

"Fine," she said. "But if I miss something, I'm gonna know who to blame."

He grinned. "Deal."

They walked through the warehouse toward the door. Some sections were busy and some were totally empty. A large part of Frederick's organization was deployed at the protest, and headquarters felt oddly empty. A cook banked up coals in the massive barbecue. Penelope's hacker squadron was hard at work. But the fighting pit was vacant, and the logistics team was absent too.

When they reached the door, Henok put a hand on her shoulder and squeezed.

"You've been through a lot in the last few days," he said. "Don't forget how much of a difference your efforts have made. What you've done required far more bravery and creativity than I've ever been able to muster. I'm honored to have partnered with you to tell this story. I just wish it didn't have to be a tragedy."

She shrugged. "All I did was take the pictures in the first place," she said. "I couldn't have done any of the rest of it alone."

"And we couldn't have done it without you."

The dogs mobbed her as she crossed the asphalt, a storm of pink tongues and wet noses. Maybe it was time she liquidated the Trust Fund. She had spent years contributing to it and daydreaming of the exotic locales she would one day be able to document. But the last few days had proved that she didn't need to travel in order to seek adventure. There was more adventure than she could stomach right here in Oakland. She scratched the fur on one of the dog's heads. Adventure had just been a proxy anyway. What she had really been after was purpose.

Maybe she could turn her lens inward. She could use the savings to finance herself to follow local stories until she was able to earn commissions for them. She and Henok could chase down investigative leads and blow open more conspiracies. Though, to be fair, they hadn't even gotten to the bottom of *this* conspiracy yet. Now that their findings were public, it was only a matter of time before someone apprehended the man. Once they did, there would be so many more questions to be answered. The more she thought about it, the more she realized she really did need to rest.

A Fleet was waiting when she reached the sidewalk. One of the guards held the door open. They were the only two enforcers she'd seen at the Compound since her first visit. The others must be out at the protest.

She sank into the backseat of the Fleet, and the door clicked shut behind her. It was so comfortable. She ordered it to her home address, and the vehicle pulled smoothly away from the curb. Every time she blinked, she had to force her eyes open again. It would take less than ten minutes to get home. Maybe she could just let them close. She'd wake up at her front door.

On the next blink, she didn't fight it. She drifted into the satiny embrace of sleep.

35

THE CHOPPER MADE A SMOOTH CURVE around the massive tower of black smoke rising from the bonfire that still blazed in the middle of the intersection. Once clear, its nose dipped, and it came in at a sharp angle. This had the dual benefit of accelerating them for a fast pass and maximizing visibility through the front view screens.

"Accounts differ," said Karl. He had taken manual control of the chopper once they had reached the tactical zone. "But my analysts have already reviewed the footage. The size of the protest is beginning to surge again, and they've been right at the line all night, pushing up against our officers. A bunch of teenagers started throwing bricks at the riot cops holding the line. Not that big of a deal. They just used their shields to deflect them. But then another kid came forward with what looked like a gun. When he raised it, a sniper setup on top of the highway took him out. Then the gangbangers opened up, and it's going downhill from there."

A strange mix of terror and sorrow welled up inside Huian. This was her home. Despite all their efforts at de-escalation, it was devolving into violence. "The kid," she said. "Did he actually shoot anyone?"

Karl grimaced but his eyes remained on the flight path. "We don't have 100 percent confirmation yet, but my analysts think it was a water pistol painted to look real."

"Jesus Christ." To her own ears, Huian's voice sounded like it was coming from kilometers away. "Jesus fucking Christ."

Karl's jaw clenched. "I've ordered my men to stand down but... Well, fuck. You can see it for yourself. That's why we're here against my better judgment." Huian had insisted they do a fly-by. Cumulus's drones, cameras, and sensors had extraordinary coverage, but sometimes there was no substitute for being there in person.

The chopper was swooping low over the protest to the intersection of 40th Street and Highway 24. Muzzles flashed from all directions, and they could hear the pop-pop-pop of automatic weapons fire over the sound of the rotor. The riot officers barricaded under the freeway had thrown tear-gas canisters into the crowd. The white gas billowed and swirled, tracers zipping through cloud. But someone had been distributing gas masks, and most people in the crowd were already wearing them. Frederick's dreadlocked enforcers had fortified many of the buildings on the Fringe side of Highway 24, and were laying down cover fire on the snipers holed up behind the guardrails. Where Security had painted their line, 40th Street was complete chaos. Corpses bled out on the asphalt. Media drones buzzed everywhere, delivering live feeds to the mesmerized internet masses. Chandra must have been having a heart attack.

Karl brought them around for another pass. A Molotov cocktail spiraled through the air and exploded against the shield of a riot officer. Something small and dark flashed over the chaotic maelstrom of the line and under the overpass. Another followed. Huian tried to see where it was coming from and saw a boy with a rusty red wagon filled with what looked like rocks. He was firing them one after another out of an oversized slingshot. Blinding light flashed from beneath the overpass, and fire gouted out either side and up through the BART tracks that separated the two sections of highway. Bodies tumbled everywhere. The shock wave made the chopper shudder and jump, and Huian bit her tongue hard. Secondary explosions roared, and the entire overpass trembled and then collapsed in a massive cloud of dust and rubble, sucking in screaming snipers from above and crushing the ranks of riot police beneath. The crowd surged forward into the confusion, clambering over the debris pile and into the Green Zone. Enforcers led the vanguard, and the Security officers and vehicles who had been stationed farther up 40th Street opened fire.

"Fuck," said Karl, cutting the chopper at a steep angle and accelerating back toward San Francisco. "Ma'am, I must insist we return to base. I cannot guarantee your safety in the air, and the National Guard will doubtless arrive soon."

Huian nodded mutely. That little boy couldn't have been more than twelve years old. Reality was tearing apart at the seams.

"You said that the number of people marching began another increase this morning," she said. "Why? What triggered it?"

Karl checked the latest reports from his analysts. "Looks like another blog post. Same anonymous author. It's a follow-up to the article from yesterday. It's exploding on social right now."

Huian pulled up the URL on a side screen and began to read.

No. It couldn't be.

Huian knew exactly what the story was describing. The Ghost Program. *Between us lies a sacred buffer, a line we should never cross. Just do your job and let me do mine.* Graham had been the one who murdered Sara Levine and set off this entire powder keg. Not only that, he'd been discovered and followed. Even worse, someone was reverse-engineering the architecture of the Ghost Program algorithms. One way or the other, it would inevitably lead them to Cumulus. Which meant that Graham was threatening Cumulus. Her most trusted adviser was undermining her magnum opus, sabotaging the future she had devoted her life to building.

She glanced up, trying to keep herself from hyperventilating. The chopper was skimming across the bay. Something was hanging from the lower deck of the bridge. Some kind of banner.

"Stop," she said.

"Ma'am," said Karl. "We need to get back to headquarters."

Huian gave him the full force of her stare. "Stop this chopper right now and get us closer to whatever that thing is." She pointed. "If you don't, I will personally destroy every fucking pinball machine in your basement with a baseball bat."

His nostrils flared, but he brought the chopper around and settled it into a hover. It stirred up the surface of the bay beneath it, throwing up a curtain of fine spray.

"That motherfucker," said Huian. Her voice was so soft it was nearly inaudible over the rotors.

Karl looked up, incredulous. "Is that... Is that Graham Chandler?"

"That motherfucker," she said again. The football-field-sized banner of Graham's face rippled in the wind thrown off by the chopper. His cover was blown, and her company with it. She should never have hired him. She should never have given him so much autonomy. She should never have authorized the Ghost Program in the first place. He had gone so much further than she could ever have imagined. *Don't send errand boys to manipulate me.* He must be behind that, too. That's why Martín had come in this morning looking like he'd seen a ghost and offering up Tectonix on a silver platter. *I'm not the kind of person who's willing to throw his own daughter to the dogs. So take my company, ravage my life's work.* What else had Graham been doing that Huian didn't even know about?

"Bring us in over the bridge," she said. The article mentioned that other photos were everywhere.

Karl increased their altitude and flew slowly into San Francisco with the surface of the Bay Bridge beneath them.

There he was, plastered over every single fucking billboard. Exiting Sara's house. Entering the BART station. Patronizing a café.

"Stop." Her voice was a harsh whisper.

This time, Karl didn't question the order.

The billboard showed Graham closing the door of a small office building, a smug smile on his face. Huian knew that building. She had been there too many times with Vera for sessions that only ever made things worse. Shiny bald spots and potted plants. She hated that place. She hated Dr. Corvel.

What the fuck was Graham doing at his office?

36

THE WORLD BLURRED BACK INTO FOCUS. Something had woken Lilly. She must be home. But the Fleet wasn't parked. Instead, it was accelerating up an incline. The change in angle had shaken her awake.

It took her a moment to scramble back up the slope to consciousness. She had left Henok to get some rest. It had been more than thirty hours since she'd slept. She'd nodded off in the Fleet en route to her apartment. But she lived less than ten minutes from Frederick's warehouse. So where exactly was she?

Outside the window, she saw wide lanes and thick cables rising up to a central pylon. Wind-ruffled water stretched out to either side. A bridge. The Bay Bridge. What the hell was she doing on the Bay Bridge heading toward San Francisco? You didn't even have to get on the freeway to make your way from the warehouse to her apartment. Had she butt-dialed a new destination for the Fleet? Or slept for so long in the backseat of the vehicle that it reset to pick up a new passenger?

She pulled out her phone and swiped her finger across the screen. It didn't respond. She tried again, but again there was no response. Depressing a button flush with the edge, she restarted it. Nothing. Shit. Had she forgotten to charge it last night?

She'd been up all night hitching rides on trucks to and from the warehouse to distribute and install the photos all over the city. Maybe her battery had run out of juice. She couldn't remember the last time she'd checked how much charge remained. What was the protocol for a Fleet rider whose phone died? Surely, the system still knew her destination and charged her account automatically anyway. There was no way their engineers hadn't accounted for that eventuality—it must happen every day. So then where the hell was this thing taking her?

Across the water, the skyscrapers of downtown San Francisco gleamed in the morning light. The Bay Bridge started in Oakland, landed on Treasure Island where the lanes dove into a tunnel, and then arced up again on the other side all the way to the San Francisco Embarcadero. Like all the Cumulus companies, Fleet was headquartered on their otherworldly Presidio campus. Maybe she was headed for some kind of maintenance lot.

The control panel. She should have thought of it right away. That was the problem with operating on so little sleep—it decelerated your thinking. Each Fleet vehicle was equipped with a dashboard interface where you could manually adjust speaker volume for music, map your route, and whatever else it was you needed. She could just check that and adjust the parameters to get her back home. She might even be able to submit a ticket to customer support and find out why she'd been sent on a wild goose chase to begin with.

Treasure Island rose up in front of the windshield, the road diving into the dark maw of the tunnel burrowing through it. She scooted forward to one of the front seats and tapped the panel. Her own reflection stared back at her from a dark screen. She touched the panel again, leaving her index finger on it for a few extra seconds to make sure the sensors registered. The screen stayed blank. Her stomach tightened, and a bead of cold sweat trickled down her spine. This definitely wasn't normal.

She was thrown back against the seat as the car made a sharp left turn. Sticking out an arm, she braced herself before she lost her seat. She hadn't put on a seatbelt after moving up here. She'd been so focused on the dashboard, she hadn't been looking out the windshield at where they were going. Now she peered out through the windows, trying to get her bearings.

The Fleet had taken the left exit onto Treasure Island. Now it was curving around the island on a narrow road that was wet with morning dew. Trees flashed past on either side. No other cars were visible.

Lilly punched every button on the dashboard. Panic ripened in her gut. Nothing was responding. She couldn't even turn on the damn radio. Changing tactics, she tried to open her window. But the glass didn't budge. She yanked the door handle, trying to open it even as the car rounded a corner and passed over the San Francisco side of the bridge. The door was locked. She pulled at the lock mechanism but it stayed in place. The Fleet had locked her in. She pried at it, but only managed to crack a fingernail. Fuck, that hurt. She sucked the blood that oozed from it.

She was trapped. Scrambling to the back of the vehicle she pounded her fists on the rear window and shouted for help. But the passengers flying by on the bridge below her couldn't hear or see her and receded into the distance as the Fleet negotiated down the north slope of the island. It dropped into an area that was filled with waterfront warehouses and industrial buildings. Treasure Island had been a naval facility before the land and facilities were sold off. Fears of toxic contamination had held back the tide of ambitious real-estate developers that had colonized the rest of the Bay Area.

Something was very wrong. Wherever this Fleet was headed, she didn't want to go. If she punched out the window, she could wait for the car to slow and then squeeze through it and try not to kill herself when she hit the ground. Wait. If she punched out the windows, she'd probably cut her hands to shreds. Better to kick. Her feet were more protected and legs were stronger anyway.

She slid onto the back seats and lay on her back with her feet propped up against the far door. She could feel the Fleet making a turn and ascending a short ramp. Enough of this bullshit. She tensed her core, pressed her palms into the door behind her for leverage, and kicked the opposite window with all her might. Pain jolted up through her heels. Damn, the window was strong. Pulling her feet back, she kicked again. And again. And again. On the third kick, something gave, and a fractal network of cracks appeared in the glass. She was breathing heavily. One more would do it. This time, her feet went clear through and the window crumbled into nuggets of safety glass.

The Fleet came to a smooth stop. Lilly pushed herself up to a sitting position. All four doors opened of their own accord. Then everything went insane. The horn blared in a randomized pattern. All the interior and exterior lights and the dashboard monitor flashed with seizure-inducing rapidity. The seats reclined and straightened. The engine revved. Hot air blasted from every vent. Death metal roared from the speakers at maximum volume and pain seared through Lilly's eardrums.

Raising her hands to cover her ears and squinting to keep out the lights, Lilly threw herself from the deranged vehicle. A grunt escaped her as her shoulder hit cement. Rolling onto her back, she scooted away from the Fleet on her ass, trying to put distance between herself and the madness. Some removed corner of her mind hoped that this was all some kind of mental breakdown, that the psychosis was in her head and not her environment.

Then her shoulders hit two poles, stopping her retreat. No, not poles. Legs. One of her hands butted up against the edge of a shoe. All light and sound from the Fleet ceased, leaving an eerie silence in their wake. She tilted her head back, looking up.

Her heart froze in her chest, and the smell of bougainvillea flooded her sense memory.

"I would apologize again for being forward," said Sara's killer, his expression mild. "But it appears you were the one who had me at a disadvantage."

37

GRAHAM TORE the duct tape from her mouth. It left behind a red rectangle of irritated skin around her full lips.

"Frederick O'Livier." Her voice shook as badly as her body.

He looked down his nose at her. Plucking up a pair of surgical scissors from the side table, he cut loose her T-shirt and bra, and let the fragments fall to the floor. Goose bumps prickled on her pale skin. He unscrewed a small jar and dipped a finger in to scoop up some gel. Reaching out, he gently rubbed the gel onto each of her nipples. Oh, how he wished the circumstances were different. Her areolae were dark against the soft mound of each breast. He felt himself stiffen against his jeans. She struggled to twist out of his way, but plastic zip ties secured her wrists, elbows, and ankles to the steel chair that stood alone on the open expanse of concrete floor.

"I swear to God," she said, tears streaming down her cheeks. "I'm telling you the truth."

Ignoring her, Graham attached electrodes to each nipple. The conductive gel would ensure a good connection. He wiped his hands off on a neatly folded towel and ran a finger along the line of her jaw. Her eyes were wide open, but to her credit, she didn't flinch.

"Lilly." He shook his head. "You must forgive my skepticism.

Perhaps I'm simply close-minded, but I have a hard time believing a slumlord like Frederick O'Livier would be the man pulling the strings behind your little, ah... *project*. He certainly has a knack for drug distribution and community engagement. But I can't seem to imagine him running an op this complex."

Her face twisted. "What do you *mean*? I saw you leaving Sara's and followed you because I knew you'd shot her. That's it. That's all. Frederick paid for all the billboards and stuff. But that was afterwards. Once I met him and Henok."

In a flash, he had his hand at her throat and thrust his face toward her so that their noses were only a few centimeters apart.

"*Are you working for the Agency?*" He injected every ounce of poison he could muster into the words.

She shook her head, unable to speak. His eyes searched hers as her pupils dilated. He saw fear there. But not duplicity. He needed to keep his emotions out of this conversation. This was an interrogation. He was a professional. He knew how to extract information. He had once broken a KGB-trained agent. In the end, the man had begged Graham for the opportunity to reveal their operational intel. He would deconstruct Lilly's mind one phobia and nerve ending at a time. Whoever it was who was trying to stab him in the back didn't know how dangerous it was to cross him. They may have succeeded in co-opting his plans, but he could still drag them kicking and screaming to the grave alongside him.

Releasing her throat, he straightened and considered his options.

The flicker of her eyes gave him a quarter second of warning.

"Freeze!"

But Graham had already snatched his sidearm from the table and dropped into a crouch. Lilly was the only cover. He torqued his body around the chair and popped behind her to look over her shoulder with the gun to her temple.

"Help." Lilly tried to scream, but it came out as more of a croak.

Two figures had ducked under the wide corrugated-steel door at the end of the warehouse where Lilly's Fleet had entered earlier. The horizontal bar of morning light that entered the empty warehouse under the door backlit them so that Graham couldn't make them out clearly. They were shadows against the glare.

"Drop the weapon and raise your hands." A man shouted. He knew that voice. What was his name? Karl. Karl Dieter.

As they approached, Graham's eyes adjusted and—fuck. Karl strode forward, keeping his pistol trained on Graham. Huian walked beside him, black leather flight jacket over designer blouse and slacks. He had never seen such intensity packed into a stare. Why the hell were Karl and Huian here? How had they found him? Could she have revoked his Ghost Program privileges and geolocated him? This situation was deteriorating rapidly. He just needed a little time. Enough to sort things out and create a new set of contingencies.

"Stop right there or she dies," said Graham and felt Lilly stiffen.

"Lilly?" Huian looked down at his hostage in astonishment. Then her eyes perused the screws, scalpels, electrodes, car batteries, chemicals, hypodermic needles, and other bits of espionage accoutrement arrayed on the table.

"Huian!" Lilly gasped. "Get me out of here. My Fleet went crazy, he kidnapped me with it and brought me—"

It was Graham's turn to do a double-take. They *knew* each other. They knew each other. And here was Huian showing up with her pet mall cop in tow. Dominos started to fall. His erection wilted, and bile rose in his throat. He had underestimated her. The whole time he had thought Huian was oblivious to how he was subverting her organization. She always focused on the surface of things, never tried to read between the lines. He had trusted that analysis because it resonated with the other engineers he'd worked with. Earnest people who took problems at face value and immediately focused on finding solutions rather than seeking advantage. But the whole time she'd been running a counterintelligence op against him, keeping him in check. With one hand, she'd signed off on the Ghost Program, and with the other, she'd signed Lilly as an agent to track him and report back on his activities. Lilly must have found some way to report her location to Huian.

"Honey," said Huian. "Slow down."

"Shut the fuck up," said Graham. "Both of you."

Huian's gaze snapped back to him, twin almond-shaped infernos.

"I said, drop the weapon." Karl's voice was strained.

Without looking, Huian placed a calming hand on his shoulder.

"You," she said to Graham. She let the word hang in the air for a moment where it accrued layers of inference like a magnet attracting metal shavings. "Leave the poor woman alone and tell me what the *fuck* you've done."

Graham's laugh was higher pitched than he wanted it to be. "Oh, come on," he said. "Lilly's no innocent. She's working for you. You've had her following me for who knows how long. We're all grown-ups here. She needs to deal with the consequences of her actions."

Huian's eyes narrowed. "If that's what you actually think, then paranoia really has gotten the better of you. You think Lilly was acting on *my* orders? Then, pray tell, why the fuck would I have told her to put Cumulus at risk by writing a Ghost Program exposé and pasting your pathetic face all over the damn city?"

Graham didn't have an answer for that. His arm ached where he had mutilated it with the shard of cereal bowl. His breath came hot and fast. Lilly's hair smelled like smoke.

"Now," said Huian. "What the hell were you doing with Dr. Corvel?"

Graham stared at her for a moment. Her question confirmed her story. The biggest tech mogul in history really didn't have a clue. No counterintelligence after all. He still found the hubris startling. People wielded immense power with so little regard for security. If she didn't know how he'd coerced Corvel, then maybe his insurance plan was still intact. He could spring his trap and finally put a leash on Huian. Lilly had destroyed his cover and trashed his plans, but he could still flee and pull Cumulus's strings from an overseas safe house. He could hold Cumulus hostage just as he now held Lilly.

"You will arrange for a private jet to deliver me to Mexico City this afternoon," said Graham. "You will hold a press conference and announce that this was a new kind of cybersecurity breach by an unknown party." His voice gained confidence as his words created their own momentum. "You will promise to conduct an in-depth investigation, which Karl will lead. I will supply the evidence you need to demonstrate that Sara was killed by someone hurt by one of her previous cases. Your investigation will conclude that the killer was himself murdered in a bar fight in Tijuana. I will provide the evidence there as well. You will both leave now so that I can dispose of this particular loose end." He jammed the barrel of the pistol into Lilly temple, and she hissed. "I will issue additional orders once this is settled."

Karl and Huian glanced at each other.

"You don't seem to understand what's going on here," said Huian. "You're going to release Lilly, and Karl is going to take you into custody."

Graham smiled blandly. Time to drop the bomb. "If you do not follow my instructions to the letter, I will release a package of information that will make WikiLeaks look like child's play. VIP sex tapes recorded via their Cumulus devices. Don't worry—I've got a good mix of politicians, business leaders, religious authorities, and celebrities. Cumulus source code and terabytes of trade secrets. Once it's out there, there's no going back. The names, addresses, and financial, employment, and medical records of every single employee. You might be facing quite a bit of talent flight after that. Your entire M&A deal history and communications, thanks to Richard." He shook his head. "You really should be nicer to people, you know. Vera's and your entire set of case files with Dr. Corvel. His unfortunate stash of child porn, and transcripts of how he intentionally sabotaged your marriage on my orders. I must say, there's some seriously personal stuff in there. Your parents really should have been more interested in you and less obsessed with the glory they left behind in Jakarta. You should have been more considerate of Vera, though. Just because she's not consumed by projects like you are, she doesn't deserve to be ignored. Oh, even Martín's daughter enjoying a collegiate three-some, and how he played both his own board and Cumulus." His smile sharpened. "Last but not least, full recordings of every single operation I've ever run for Cumulus. The Ghost Program stopped Cumulus from recording me, but I always traveled with a camera and have the entire history stored on off-network hard drives. The intrigue will be scintillating. It was just an insurance policy, and now I'm glad I've been paying my premiums. Just in case you haven't been paying attention, Cumulus will be destroyed beyond any hope of resuscitation, and you'll go to prison as a collaborator."

Huian swayed on her feet and then slowly lowered herself to her knees, placing both palms onto the floor to steady herself. A thousand-mile stare dowsed the fire in her eyes. Her breath came in short gasps. She pressed her forehead onto the cold concrete, and her entire body trembled like a leaf in an autumn breeze.

Karl looked down at her in concern and confusion. Then his attention snapped back to Graham. "Save your testimony for the prosecutors," said Karl. "Drop the weapon and step away from her, or I swear to God I'll double-tap you in the head."

Graham winked. "You might want to ask your boss before doing that," he said. "If I fail to check in for three days in a row, the package automatically sends itself to every major news outlet. My death would seriously hamper my ability to prevent this unfortunate occurrence. You know how leaks can be."

Trap sprung.

An invisible weight lifted from Graham's shoulders. It was such a relief to close the loop on his plans. This wasn't how he had envisioned it culminating, but life always threw curve balls. Now that it was all out in the open, he wouldn't have to dance around Huian anymore. The legendary executive was shivering where she knelt on the floor. She was nothing but his puppet now. Lilly had exposed him. It was too late to fix that. His former masters at the Agency and anyone who actually knew him would recognize his face. He was already iterating the plan. He couldn't frame someone else for Sara's murder. He'd have to manufacture a motive and fake his own death. Then he would retreat into the shadows and become a hard target, directing Cumulus from afar.

Huian raised her head from the floor. Silent tears streamed down her face. Her lips were a thin line. She looked ten years older.

"What do you want?" she asked. Her voice was hollow, bereft of feeling.

"I told you what I want. We'll start with that list and go from there."

Her face contorted in a flash of rage that she immediately suppressed. "No," she said. "That's bullshit. That's logistics." She spat on the concrete next to her and wiped the tears from her cheeks with a sleeve. "You've murdered, blackmailed, and manipulated every single human you've encountered just to hijack my company. You started a civil war in the streets of Oakland. You're about to torture an innocent person to death. You've sacrificed your own humanity and gone to unimaginable lengths to engineer this... this spectacle of horrors. Why? What do you *want*? What could possibly be worth this?"

Graham opened his mouth but nothing came out. He was... empty.

What *did* he want? The question flitted through his head like a sparrow in an auditorium that couldn't find a place to perch. *The first rule of espionage was to find leverage over your boss.* The intricacies of following that line to its logical extreme had demanded his full attention. He had never allowed himself the opportunity to consider what might happen if he actually succeeded. The Agency's labyrinthine bureaucracy had made the answer self-evident. Success earned you a new boss higher up the totem pole, and you immediately got back to business. Even the director had to follow the president's orders. Granddad and his surviving colleagues had always bitched about the onion of federal red tape. That was one of the reasons Graham had made his move to Silicon Valley. The lack of red tape here had made his coup that much more effective. In one fell swoop, he had just crowned himself a dark prince of the internet.

But instead of the expected satisfaction of fulfilled ambition, unadulterated terror flooded through him. His tongue felt sticky and dry in his mouth. His arm throbbed. His heart threatened to burst from his chest. Now that he finally had it in his grasp, he had no idea whatsoever what to do with this newfound power. There was too much uncertainty. There were too many factors to consider. Without a compass, how could he direct his prize? Any action he took would expose Cumulus and himself to a nearly infinite array of risk factors. And inaction was action. It was paralyzing. It transformed life into a halting problem with no solution. Every move cascaded into unseen contingencies born of interaction effects.

Granddad had always served a cause higher than himself. At the end of the day, that's why he grumbled about idiot politicians, but still believed American democracy was worth defending. However critical, he was never cynical. Graham had idolized him. Only now did he know why. Service was ennobling, not demeaning. Granddad wasn't a prince. He was an agent.

And Graham was too.

Dread gave Graham a sudden sense of clarity. In just the last five minutes, he had believed with complete certainty that Lilly had been surveilling him, first on the Agency's orders and then on Huian's orders, before realizing how preposterous it all was. His own mind was oscillating like a metronome between fantastical extremes. Ever since leaving the Agency, he had enmeshed himself in a byzantine lattice of rationalization that was starting to collapse. *Here in San Francisco, he was a wolf among lambs.* It had been too easy for a reason. He wasn't embedded in some kind of overseas insurgency. He was manipulating American civilians. They were *supposed* to be lambs. That was the whole point. He had been subverting the way of life he had sworn to protect. An oath he had betrayed out of juvenile disappointment that the world hadn't lived up to his expectations.

He looked at the goose bumps along the pale line of Lilly's naked neck. He had murdered a lawyer who had dedicated her career to fighting corporate corruption. He had threatened children and blackmailed without restraint. He had destroyed relationships and interfered with geopolitics for private gain. He had hijacked America's most prominent company and crippled its founder. He had turned Oakland into an urban war zone. He had been about to torture a photographer to satisfy his own paranoid sense of vengeance. Not an enemy soldier or double agent. A curious photographer.

He snorted and Karl twitched. Without any counterintelligence training, Lilly had broken his cover wide open despite his years of covert operations and impossibly high digital defenses. Hubris made power a self-limiting function.

The trap he had built wasn't for Huian. It was for himself. The barefoot boy with the binoculars rose from the ashes of memory.

Graham raised the gun and pulled the trigger.

38

THE SHOT RANG through the desolate expanse of the empty warehouse, echoing Huian's shattered life.

She and Karl sprinted forward. She went straight to Lilly, kneeling in front of her chair.

"Are you okay?" Huian raised her voice. The gun had gone off less than a meter from Lilly, and her ears must be ringing. There were no bruises or burn marks on her exposed upper body.

Lilly nodded, eyes wild and cheeks wet. "Yeah," she said. "He didn't have time to actually... do anything to me. What happened?" She craned her neck to peer back over her shoulder.

Karl looked up at Huian from where he knelt by Graham's body. "He's dead," he said. "The man knew how to shoot to kill."

Huian tried to absorb what she had learned in the last few minutes. Groovy jazz piano scales danced in her memory. Thick brown hair tumbling over the shoulders of a baby-blue summer dress. The smell of citrus and wet earth. *Honey, there's no easy way to say this. I want a divorce.* Graham had driven a wedge between her and Vera, prying them apart so he could isolate and manipulate Huian. Her mind recoiled from even thinking about it. Their divorce had been a masterful move in a game where they were all his pawns. She had never felt so... violated.

Anger flared, and she swiped at the tears she couldn't stop from falling. She needed to keep the emotional turmoil raging inside her under control. Situations like this didn't allow for margins of error.

"Check in with your staff," she said to Karl. "We need an update on the protest. We can deal with this mess later. Oh, and give me your knife."

He gestured acknowledgment, tossed her a multitool, and stepped away.

She flicked out a serrated blade and sawed through the plastic zip ties that bound Lilly to the chair. Then she helped her remove the electrodes and wipe the gel away with a fragment of the destroyed T-shirt. Lilly was shivering in the chill of the warehouse. Shrugging the flight jacket off her shoulders, Huian helped Lilly into it, and then zipped up the front. Luckily, he hadn't removed or destroyed her pants or shoes.

Lilly exhaled slowly. "Who was he?" She stared at the body lying in a pool of rapidly congealing blood. The bullet had opened a ragged hole in the right side of Graham's jaw and exited via the back-left side of his skull. His eyes were open and vacant.

The words hung in the air for a moment.

"His name was Graham Chandler," said Huian. He hadn't looked like much when he had first ventured into her office. Yet another corporate flunky hoping to add Cumulus to his résumé. But then he revealed he had duped their entire recruiting team, and his very presence in her office proved that Cumulus needed his talents. Huian had built the company from the ground up. Digging ditches required gumption that senior managers often forgot or had never learned in the first place. She'd respected Graham's approach, and since that day, he had earned more and more of her trust and time. Until today. She sighed. "He worked for me. Or, at least, he was supposed to. It turns out he was only ever working for himself."

"He killed Sara," said Lilly. It was a statement, not a question.

Take care of them. If only real life had do-overs. Huian was just as responsible for Sara's death as Graham was.

"Ma'am," Karl had his hand over his phone. "The governor is at our headquarters. He's demanding to see you immediately. The White House has aides waiting on the line, and half the company is trying to get ahold of you. The FBI has a team of investigators throwing warrants at my personnel. The National Guard is deploying and should have the fighting under control within the next few hours. We need to go."

They ducked under the partially open steel door. The morning sunlight was blinding after the gloom of the warehouse. Weeds sprang up from cracks in the sidewalk. Tendrils of evaporating dew rose from the asphalt as the street began to warm. A few blocks away, a flock of seagulls circled over the bay. The tranquility of the scene belied the catastrophe Graham had wrought. Looking east, Huian saw smoke billowing into the blue skies over Oakland.

Everything she had worked for was going up in flames. Huian had devoted her life to building Cumulus. Vera had been right. It was the center of her world. All her relationships, all her ideas, all her fears were forever enmeshed in the company. Now, her darkest unspoken nightmare had come to fruition. Her dream had been subverted. Her baby would be taken away from her. Graham had made good on every promise he had ever made to her. He had fixed the China problem. He'd secured the mission-critical competitive intelligence she needed. He'd excavated skeletons in the closets of potential hires and kept her abreast of internal power struggles. Now, she wondered how much of that had been manufactured. The only thing she knew for sure was that she couldn't afford to ignore his final promise.

It would shape the rest of her life.

39

DOWNDRAFT SET THEIR HAIR STREAMING and eyes watering as the Fleet chopper touched down in the middle of the empty road on Treasure Island. It had dropped Huian and Karl off a few blocks away, far enough that the sound hadn't alerted Graham to their presence. Since then, it had circled far overhead, waiting to pick them up.

They jogged out, boarded, and got themselves strapped in. Karl helped Lilly with the restraints.

"I've never been in one of these before," she said, running her fingertips along the glass of one of the windows.

"I'll get us moving back to HQ," Karl said to Huian.

"No, wait." She held up a hand and turned to Lilly. "I need to talk to Frederick O'Livier. Can you tell us where we can find him?"

Lilly frowned but, after a moment, nodded. "I don't know whether to blame you for Sara's death or thank you for saving my life," she said. "But as long as you promise no harm will come to Frederick, I can bring you to him."

"You have my word," said Huian.

"Ma'am," said Karl, frustration edging into his tone. "We have to get back. The president has an open line waiting for you, and the governor has been screaming at Tom for an hour."

"Then they'll have to wait," she said. "There isn't much time, and they're not very high on my list of priorities."

The chopper leapt into the air, pressing them all back into their seats. Backwash from the rotors kicked up spray from the surface of the bay as they accelerated out across the water. They gained altitude, and soared over the eastern half of the Bay Bridge. Dozens of cables extended from the single central pylon to support the wide arc of steel and concrete. Loading cranes squatted on the Port of Oakland. From this height, they could see muzzle flashes, smoke, and explosions from the ongoing battle at MacArthur. National Guard helicopters had joined the cloud of Security and news drones circling in the surrounding airspace, and soldiers were rappelling down to enter the fray.

Huian remembered a ballpoint pen sitting on a single piece of paper marooned on the wide granite surface of their kitchen island. *I'm tired of being an externality.* She smiled sadly. Graham may have orchestrated their separation, but Dr. Corvel, for all that Huian hated him, had only cultivated seeds that had been planted long before. The president and the governor weren't high on her list of priorities. But when push came to shove, Vera wasn't either. Huian loved her, but the mission subsumed such personal obligations. *The future was a demanding mistress.* If Huian was going to define it, she had to pay the price. Over and over again.

Her eyes traced the border that separated the Green Zone from the Slums. That line was about to become more porous. Her vision of a perfect utopia would be diluted by the festering mud of democratic social reality. *Whenever wealth is so unevenly distributed in a population, social tension is bound to arise. When social tension grows, protests and other forms of unrest simply become a part of the fabric of the nation.* Graham hadn't had any moral high ground to stand on, but the success of his methods proved his point. For a fleeting moment he had commandeered Cumulus, an accomplishment on par with a national coup. But he hadn't needed an army. All he had needed was to get to her. The company was too reliant on her. She might have dedicated her life to building the future, but the future couldn't depend on her. Through careful management of board composition, voting rights, and equity dilution, she had ensured that she remained firmly in control of Cumulus. That had given her the authority to be agile in a world of lethargic institutions, and go boldly where others balked. But it had also made her a critical point of failure. Good leaders made themselves indispensable. Great leaders made themselves expendable. Conflating the two had nearly cost her everything.

Under Lilly's direction, the chopper touched down in an industrial section of West Oakland adjacent to the port. Two dreadlocked men stationed on the sidewalk aimed assault rifles at them as they stepped down onto the pavement. But they lowered their guns when they recognized Lilly. A pack of pit bulls slavered behind a high fence surrounding the Compound. A massive warehouse rose in the middle of it all, brightly colored murals covering its walls.

"We've got business with Frederick," she told them. "Let him know I'm coming in with Huian Li and Karl Dieter."

"You gonna walk 'em back?"

"Yeah."

Huian and Karl looked at Lilly in surprise as she stepped between them and took their hands. Her palm was small and warm against Huian's. The men opened the gate, and Huian half expected the dogs to tear them to pieces. Instead, the pack parted and wet tongues lapped at her as they walked hand-in-hand to the warehouse.

The door opened just as they arrived.

"Lilly!" A slender young man charged out. "I've been trying to call you for over an hour to tell you about what's happening at MacArthur. I knew you wouldn't want to sleep through it, but I couldn't get through to your phone. Are you okay?"

Lilly smiled. "I'm all right, Henok," she said. "I'll tell you all about it later. But right now, we've got to see Frederick."

Henok's eyes widened. "He's waiting for you in the conference room. He has the mayor with him."

Karl snorted, but Huian shot him a warning look.

Henok and Lilly escorted them through a cavernous interior that housed everything from boxing rings and cubicle farms to pit barbecues. Dozens of people looked up from their various activities to glance over at the newcomers, but nobody paid them undue attention. Huian would have been impressed, but the day's events had dulled her capacity for amazement. They negotiated a labyrinth of pathways, and entered a large sunken conference room that was walled off from the rest of the space.

The half-dozen people seated at the central table stood as their group descended from the door. Huian recognized the likeably chubby mayor of Oakland, Juan Gonzalez. His hair was combed back with liberal use of gel, and his cheap suit was fraying at the edges. He had two young members of his staff with him. Her eyes traveled up to meet the gaze of the man at the other end of the table, Frederick O'Livier. He was a head taller than the aides at his side, his sinewy build athletic despite his age. The tuxedo complemented his aristocratic features. Despite the circumstances, she couldn't suppress a rush of fangirl nerves. The Golden State Warriors had been her private obsession since she'd been introduced to basketball on the court of the Palo Alto YMCA when she was six years old. O'Livier was a Warriors legend, and it felt surreal to be standing in the same room as him, even though she now owned the team and met NBA stars on a regular basis. Nostalgia deified role models.

"Ms. Li," Frederick's voice was smooth and resonant. "Forgive me for cutting right to the chase, but we don't have time for niceties. Did you order the assassination of Sara Levine?"

The mayor sucked in a shocked breath. The bluntness of his question took Huian off guard, and she had to take a moment to recover. On balance, it was better this way. He was right that they didn't have time for small talk.

"Sir," said Karl, outraged. "I must—"

Huian held up a hand to stop him. She composed herself and looked directly into Frederick's dark eyes. "I did," she said, and felt the full weight of the admission settle onto her shoulders. Everyone's face in the room went blank in shock except for Frederick's. He remained entirely focused on her. Everything rested on this. It must work. "At the time, I did not comprehend what I had approved or how it would be carried out. I realize that will hold no water here or anywhere else. I am not here to make excuses, or to make amends. All this and much, much more will be made public tomorrow, and I and others will be held to account. Nothing can bring Sara back. Instead, I am here to use what authority and resources remain to me to end the violence on the streets of Oakland, and to extend Cumulus services to all residents, regardless of their ability to pay. Will you hear me out?"

Perfect silence reigned. The universe seemed to orbit around their locked gaze. Sara had been his friend, lover, and confidante. Huian could only imagine the internal conflict that must be raging inside his soul. There was likely nothing he'd like more than to have one of his enforcers shoot her where she stood. On balance, that might be a less painful prospect than what tomorrow held.

After a full minute, he adjusted his bow tie. "What do you propose?" he said.

An unexpected flush of joy rushed through her. She had her chance.

"In your final game," she said, "you sucked. The Warriors depended on you to lead their offense, but you couldn't hit a shot to save your life. By the beginning of the fourth quarter, you were down twenty points. The crowd had lost all faith. People were getting up and leaving to try to beat the traffic. But with nine minutes left, against the advice of your coach and every sports analyst out there, you benched yourself and forced Walter Jackson to relieve you as point guard. The Warriors won by three points in overtime. You sacrificed your reputation to allow the team to win the championship. I was at that game. I never understood why you did it. In retrospect it was obvious—all the pundits lauded you. But in the moment? That must have been one of the hardest decisions you ever made, ending your career in obvious disgrace. But ultimately it allowed your legacy to outlive you."

She stepped down to the floor of the conference room and gripped the back of a chair, keeping her eyes on Frederick the entire time. His eyes narrowed. "I now face a similar predicament. Three days from now, there will be a leak that shares shocking and destructive information about me and certain rogue elements within my company. We do not have time to go over the details right now, but suffice it to say that the excellent investigative reporting of Henok and Lilly barely scratches the surface. It happened under my watch, and I will take full responsibility. Tomorrow, I will preempt the leak and release everything in a press conference."

"Ma'am," Karl grabbed her arm. "We don't know—"

She looked at him. "Graham made good on every promise he made to me," she said. "We simply cannot afford to take the chance that he was bluffing. This is the only way." After a moment, his fingers loosened and his hand fell away.

She turned back to Frederick. "As soon as this comes out," she said, "I will recuse myself from Cumulus, and likely spend the bulk of my time fighting an uphill legal battle. In the meantime, however, I still hold some sway. As you may know, through a combination of carefully managed dilution, board selection, and voting rights structures, I have maintained unilateral control of Cumulus. I built the company to realize a better future for this country, and the world. In so many ways, we have already succeeded. In so many other ways, we have a long way to go. I've always thought about that gap in technical terms, and tried to bridge it via investments in R&D. But William Gibson once wrote that the future is already here—it's just not evenly distributed. Nowhere is that truer than Oakland. I am loath to confess that it took a lawsuit, an outbreak of urban warfare, and an extremely personal betrayal to force me to see it. To risk sounding melodramatic, the story of Oakland is the story of America. Today, we've seen the dark side of that story. With your help, I'm hoping we can see what the flipside might look like." She raised both of her hands, palms up. "Here's what I propose. I will extend all Cumulus services to all Oakland residents, with subsidies for every income level that can't already afford them. This will require close collaboration. Nobody understands Oakland better than you. Security will need to work alongside OPD. Fleet will need to talk to AC Transit. Learning will need to integrate with the school district. You get the idea. Oakland will be the test case for making Cumulus services inclusive on a regional, and then a national and international level. There are millions of details that will have to be worked out. In fact, I'm almost positive it won't work. The most probable outcome is complete ruin. Cumulus engineering teams love the term 'perpetual beta.'" She gave the phrase air quotes. "It refers to the idea of constant experimentation that assumes a high level of implicit failure instead of trying to avert every contingency through careful planning. The logic is that careful planning doesn't work very well because both failure and opportunity arrive from unexpected directions anyway. In that sense, the idea would be for Oakland to become a socioeconomic Skunk Works. It'll be messy and awkward. But so is almost every adolescent. If it's going to happen, we have to start right now."

Frederick shook his head. Exhaustion suddenly exerted an almost gravitational pull on Huian. This was her last and only gambit to preserve her vision.

"What would stop your replacement from undoing everything you just described the moment he takes over Cumulus?" he asked.

"If they are stupid enough to compound what will already be a PR nightmare by doing that," she said, "then I'll fund it personally."

"Still, it won't work," he said. "If the scandal is as far-reaching as you claim, this will be seen as a last-minute pity play to try to win public favor." He frowned, but the expression was thoughtful rather than argumentative. "As much as I hate how exclusively Cumulus has tiered its services and business practices, there's no denying the power of the technology you've built. But this plan won't fail for lack of capital or technology. What you really need is trust."

Huian nodded tiredly. "Which is why I'm here."

"Of course," said Frederick. "You can't do it alone." He touched an index finger to his temple and cast a glance at his other team members. Finally, he looked back to Huian. "Alright," he said. "Here's how we'll do it. First, we will both call off our forces around MacArthur, and dedicate those resources to immediate emergency response efforts. Then, Cumulus, my organization, and the City will establish a formal strategic partnership to implement the plan. The triumvirate will do extensive ongoing community engagement and issue popular referendums on all key decisions. We will also set up a separate independent council to advise on the implementation of this plan, chaired by you, me, and the mayor. All three of us will step down immediately and relinquish leadership—otherwise we can't be truly independent. Without separating ourselves from our organizations, we won't have a chance of earning the trust required to prosecute such a strategy."

"I will do no such thing," said the mayor, aghast. "Oakland needs a strong hand in this moment of crisis."

Frederick stared at him for a long moment. "What Oakland needs isn't for me to say," he said. "But I can assure you of at least one thing. Oakland does *not* need corrupt politicians."

The mayor's face turned beet red. "How dare—"

"Mr. Mayor," interrupted Frederick. "We have enjoyed a long and fruitful relationship. But one thing I learned playing basketball is that sometimes opportunity can be found in the darkest of moments. This is one such time. Even if this initiative fails, Oakland's citizens will surely benefit from the experiment. Even you can see that much. You can either get on board or suffer the consequences of the details of our friendship reaching the public eye."

"Well then," said the mayor, sweat beading on his forehead.

"That's the spirit," said Frederick.

"Boss," said a woman in coveralls chewing on a pencil. "You can't leave. We need you here."

"You most certainly do not need me," said Frederick. "If I have accomplished anything over all these years, it's that." He turned to Lilly. "Ms. Miyamoto, did I not recently tell you I have been considering retirement?"

Lilly started in surprise. "Umm, yeah. You did. In the truck last night."

"I have always had a weakness for dramatic exits," said Frederick. "Ms. Li?"

"Yes?" asked Huian.

Frederick stepped forward and extended a hand.

"I hope you spend the rest of your life rotting in prison for what you've done," he said. "But you have a deal."

Huian shook. *You might discover that incredible things can happen when you relinquish control.*

It was time to put Vera's insight to the test.

40

LILLY LED HUIAN DOWN the short flight of steps that led from the alley's sidewalk to the unmarked wooden door. She opened it, and they stepped through into a cramped anteroom where they hung their coats. Then she parted the strings of hanging beads and slipped into the space beyond.

Lilly had been here so many times that this place felt like a second home. But now that she was bringing a first-time guest, she tried to see it through virgin eyes. Billowing steam and smoke rendered the air viscous with the smells of garlic, onion, and pork. The too-low ceiling gave the impression of some kind of underground speakeasy. The walls were covered in detailed illustrations of scenes that bled through the barrier of magical realism, and whispered of wild and dangerous transgression. The room was all dark wood and darker corners. Stools lined a bar on the left, and cast iron cauldrons bubbled in the open kitchen behind it. Tables hid in irregular nooks, and the entire place felt organic, as if it had grown in situ rather than being constructed by human hands. An old man in a ragged three-piece suit played a stand-up bass at the far end of the room, the rhythmic plucking providing a subconscious tempo to the low murmur of conversation.

They found a small booth in an isolated corner and squeezed in around it.

Huian was looking around in mild wonder. "I had no idea places like this existed," she said.

"You'd be surprised at the secrets hidden in the Slums," said Lilly. "Greenies think we're all missing the boat. We think you're all missing the point." This was nearly the only restaurant she ever patronized.

A teenage boy in a stained apron approached their table. Lilly held up two fingers. He nodded and disappeared back into the kitchen.

"So this is where you come when things fall apart." Huian's tone was thoughtful.

Lilly shrugged, remembering their conversation in Huian's subterranean basketball court. "Or when I need to put things back together. Or to celebrate after a successful gig. I come here when I need to process. When home doesn't have the sanctuary I need."

"Is now one of those times?"

"I'm guessing now is one of those times for both of us."

The boy returned with two massive ceramic bowls filled to the brim with ramen. The soup sloshed as he thumped them down on the table. Thick slices of pork belly and pork shoulder swam in the rich brown broth. Bright-green scallions and pickled shiitake mushrooms floated above the underlying bed of thick rice noodles. Lilly and Huian scooped up chopsticks in one hand and soup spoons in the other, and went to work. Heads bent close to the table, they slurped through the ramen with singular focus, not looking up until the bowls were empty and their bellies full.

They leaned back against the walls of the booth, and Lilly was again struck by the intensity smoldering behind Huian's eyes.

"Are you ready for tomorrow?" asked Lilly.

Huian raised her eyebrows. "I won't ever be ready for tomorrow," she said. "But that won't stop it from arriving anyway."

Sara's gruesome corpse flashed in her mind's eye. "I can't say I sympathize."

"I wouldn't expect you to. In fact, that's why I asked you to take me here."

"I was wondering why you wanted to spend your symbolic last meal with me."

"I appreciate your acquiescing."

"You saved my life today. The torturer was your employee, but still."

Lines formed around the corner of Huian's eyes but she didn't look away.

"Look," she said. "If it weren't for you, I never would have found out what Graham was really up to. He would have co-opted Cumulus and used it and me to his own ends. Whatever happens after tomorrow will be a blessing compared to that. It also high-lighted the need to separate the future of the company from my own personal fate. I can't pretend it's something I'm happy about, but it is necessary." She sucked in a deep breath through her nose. "Whatever happens, people like you and Henok will be absolutely critical. You give a voice to the voiceless. Your bravery and curiosity and disregard for what other people think are what allowed you to bring down Graham. Plus, by breaking the story wide open, you've earned the public's trust. Your conclusions will be borne out with tomorrow's announcements."

Huian ran a hand through her graying hair. "I want you to keep telling this story. Do it however you want to, in whatever format you want to. I'll give you complete access to everything I've got, and I will never turn down an interview with you. After our meeting with Frederick, I had my lawyers establish a $1 billion endowment for investigative journalism. The interest should be substantial enough to support a staff of independent reporters and editors. The endowment's evergreen, so it won't just disappear over time. You're the sole director. If you want to work with Henok, hire him. If you want to work with anyone else, do it. Do whatever you want with it. I'm hoping that plastering Graham's face all over the Bay Area was just the beginning. I obviously don't have much time to prepare for what's about to happen, but this is a critical piece of it. Frederick bankrolled your expenses, but being dependent on his patronage will shape how your work is perceived. This fund has no oversight from me or anyone else. It's just you. Make it count."

Huian stood. "Thank you, Lilly," she said. "I am truly sorry about Sara, and I owe you more than I can put into words. One day, I hope you'll allow me to make you another cocktail."

Lilly watched in stunned disbelief as Huian's retreating back disappeared through the beaded curtain. The more time she spent with Huian, the less she understood her. She had gone from seeking advantage to seeking salvation in the space of a heartbeat. *If it's going to happen, we have to start right now.* Maybe in order to build the future, you first had to forgive the present.

But what the hell was Lilly going to do with a billion dollars? She had already been dreaming of chasing down more conspiracies with Henok. Tomorrow's revelations would be a gold mine of potential stories. Thousands of leads and angles would be buried in the data. Hell, the world needed to know so much more about the battle for MacArthur and what had actually happened here over the past few days. The world needed to know what the new initiatives in Oakland meant. Were they sustainable? Were they truly independent? Would they work?

A hundred different worlds, a thousand different lives. For a moment, she was transported back to her high school photography classroom, dozens of pictures hanging at every possible angle. The acrid smell of the darkroom. Henok Addisu. She couldn't help but smile when she thought of him. The sharp lines of his face softened by the nerdy glasses. The tight curls of his dark hair and his smooth ochre skin. The abject relief on his face when she had reappeared with Huian and Karl in tow. What had Henok said when they first met? *Your story defines your identity.* She wondered what that said about her.

Lilly's first love had been photography. But maybe it wouldn't prove to be her only one after all.

THE END

THANK YOU FOR READING

I MOVED BACK to Oakland in 2013. It was the city of my birth and where I grew up. Seeing how Oakland has evolved since the '80s is at once inspiring and harrowing. *Cumulus* is a kind of twisted love letter to my favorite city in the Bay Area.

Over the course of the past few years, we've bonded with many of our incredible neighbors, sated our appetites at countless ethnic food joints, had a triple homicide on our block, installed a free little library for our community, hiked in beautiful Redwood Park, and watched a protest with thousands of people and hundreds trailing police vehicles terminate at the end of our street. We love the birdsong but hate the gunshots. Oakland feels like a special point of confluence for so many of the themes that are running hot right now: the social implications of the growing wealth gap in American society, the extraordinary promise of new technologies and diverse worldviews, our failure to solve persistent social problems like poverty, racism, and homelessness, and the power of fierce, pragmatic optimism.

Writing *Cumulus* allowed me to explore my enthusiasm for my hometown and my fascination with how new tools like the internet are reshaping our lives in so many ways, big and small. Through years of working with startups and venture capital investors, I've had the privilege of seeing how some new technologies come to be and getting to know a few of the people who build and popularize them. I've never been more excited about the promise of human ingenuity and there's no other time in history when I'd rather live. That said, these new developments are changing our social fabric, the texture of our personal lives, and even our geopolitics. Such change is always painful. Times like these require open-mindedness, compassion, critical thinking, resourcefulness, and creativity. I don't have any of the answers but I hope that in some way this story might have helped contribute a few questions.

I'm an indie author. That means I don't have a big publisher with a fancy New York office. It's just me. I hire my own editors and designers out-of-pocket. With their help, I work tirelessly to make the book the best it can possibly be. I drink a lot of coffee.

As an indie author, I'm not trying to impress an agent or please an editor. Instead, *you* are my most important partner in this creative endeavor. The success of my books depends entirely on the enthusiasm of fans and readers. Word-of-mouth is what helps people find good books. It's amazing how much of an impact you can have just by doing something simple like leaving an Amazon review, recommending the book to a friend, or sharing it on social media. So, if you enjoyed the story, pay it forward. Write a review. Mention it to someone who might like it. Make someone's day by surprising them with the gift of story. Your breath of fresh air will help fill *Cumulus*'s sails.

To get updates on my new books, reading recommendations, and behind-the-scenes details on creative process, join my author newsletter. This is the single best way to get or stay in touch with me. Emails are infrequent, personal, and substantive. I respond to every single note from folks on the mailing list. Sign up here:

www.eliotpeper.com

ACKNOWLEDGEMENTS

ALTHOUGH THERE'S ONLY ONE NAME on the cover, *Cumulus* would never have seen the light of day without the generous help of an entire team of people.

Shannon Pallone and Jesse Vernon, my tireless editors, made the prose sing and didn't let me get away with anything. Josh Anon helped brainstorm a dozen different ideas that incubated *Cumulus* and gave notes throughout the entire creative process. Tim Erickson zipped up innumerable plot holes and inconsistencies. Brad Feld, Tim O'Reilly, Lucas Carlson, Craig Lauer, and Katie Moran read early drafts and contributed invaluable input and feedback. Kevin Barrett Kane did a fabulous job designing the entire book, inside and out.

My wife, Drea Castillo, is my constant creative partner. She was a source of tireless support and tough questions that improved the story immeasurably. Our dog, Claire, kept me company and provided much-needed distractions at every opportunity.

Finally, I owe an enormous debt of gratitude to you, my fans and readers. It's hard to describe how much your attention and enthusiasm mean to me. You're a brilliant, quirky, and diverse bunch. I love reading your reviews and hearing what the stories make you think and feel. Keep reading and I'll keep writing.

ABOUT THE AUTHOR

Eliot Peper is a novelist and strategist based in Oakland, CA. He's helped build numerous technology businesses, survived dengue fever, translated Virgil's *Aeneid* from the original Latin, worked at a venture capital firm, and explored the ancient Himalayan kingdom of Mustang. When he's not writing, he works with entrepreneurs and investors to start and run companies. He loves getting lost in books, climbing rocks, surfing waves, eating chocolate, and traveling the world.

To find out more, visit his blog (www.eliotpeper.com). You can stay in touch via his author newsletter, Facebook (www.facebook.com/eliotpeper), and Twitter (@eliotpeper).

OTHER TITLES BY ELIOT PEPER:
Uncommon Stock: Exit Strategy
Uncommon Stock: Power Play
Uncommon Stock: Version 1.0